Sally Ann Hunter is a biologist and environmental policy officer. She has published a collection of poetry called *The Structure of Light* and a biography called *You Can't Keep a Good Man Down: From Parkinson's to a new life with Deep Brain Stimulation.* A paper she wrote on the biography was read on ABC Radio's *Ockham's Razor,* as was a paper on living with solar power. A number of her poems have been published in anthologies and online. She lives in the Adelaide Hills with her cat, Francis.

Sally Ann Hunter

TRANSFIGURED SEA

AUSTIN MACAULEY PUBLISHERS™
LONDON • CAMBRIDGE • NEW YORK • SHARJAH

Copyright © Sally Ann Hunter 2022

The right of Sally Ann Hunter to be identified as author of this work has been asserted by the author in accordance with section 77 and 78 of the Copyright, Designs and Patents Act 1988.

All rights reserved. No part of this publication may be reproduced, stored in a retrieval system, or transmitted in any form or by any means, electronic, mechanical, photocopying, recording, or otherwise, without the prior permission of the publishers.

Any person who commits any unauthorized act in relation to this publication may be liable to criminal prosecution and civil claims for damages.

This is a work of fiction. Names, characters, businesses, places, events, locales, and incidents are either the products of the author's imagination or used in a fictitious manner. Any resemblance to actual persons, living or dead, or actual events is purely coincidental.

A CIP catalogue record for this title is available from the British Library.

ISBN 9781786292001 (Paperback)
ISBN 9781786292704 (ePub e-book)

www.austinmacauley.com

First Published 2022
Austin Macauley Publishers Ltd®
1 Canada Square
Canary Wharf
London
E14 5AA

Coast
The Sea Sprite

The Sea Sprite's mother wades majestically out of the ocean. Her dripping dress is dark green, trailing embroidery in the same colour. She has come to gather up the Sea Sprite in her arms to take her home.

The mirrors in her heart open as if for the first time. Reflected light shines between them like sunlight on the surface of the sea.

From this radiance, she muses on the nature of the sea and the coast. The sea represents a whisper of emotions and a memory of intuition. It can be said to be the fullness of the subconscious.

The coast is a transition zone, always changing. It keeps on changing its dynamics, perpetually, in both space and time. It changes on a small scale, from waves and tides moving in and out, to currents moving along the coast with the force of the prevailing wind. Even the insubstantial wind can change direction and shape.

By these means, on a large scale, rocks wear down, cliffs are hollowed out, and sand is shifted. Even the level of the water is never the same, rising and falling as the glaciers melt or grow. It also changes on an even larger scale as sediment load makes the ocean floor move, in addition to tectonic plate margins warping and continents shifting. The exact edge of the sea cannot be delineated.

Are dreams less real because they are temporary? Or are fleeting, moving, changing things examples of their own kind of reality, a different speed? Like the sea, the sand, everything at the coast, which is moved by tides, currents, waves and winds. The sea is a dream.

In that dream, the Sea Sprite's mother resumes looking for her daughter. Although she has looked for and found the Sea Sprite before, this time she cannot find her. She wades up and down in the shallows calling for her. The sea water splashes at her ankles, the sand squelches in between her toes. There is no answer.

The sea reminds her of the interior of an abalone shell. In this light, its colours are blue, green and white.

While her feet are splashing in the water, she finds starfish and flattened sea urchins. If she looks carefully, she can see a few, scattered fish that are well camouflaged. A paper nautilus floats on the surface. This shell, created by an octopus, has a spiral shape. It reminds the mother of the fondness that the Sea Sprite has for spirals.

The mother feels inspiration in her heart because she loves the multitude of creatures belonging to the ocean. Biology has, for a long time, been her favourite way of knowing the world. Here it comes to life.

Her wet feet now take her out of the water, up to the waterlogged sand. This is where the sand doesn't dry so there are bristle worms. They are buried, except for their bristly feeding tentacles.

She moves a little higher on the beach. Where the sand is covered with water on a regular basis, she finds fan-shaped double mollusc shells. These only open when they are covered by water – otherwise, they are shut tight.

This is like some people, thinks the mother, *perhaps myself and the Sea Sprite.*

Then she walks further up, to the hard, crisp, dry sand. There remains almost no sign of life up here, but she knows that ghost crabs make burrows above the high tide line. These crabs are pale in colour, and only come out at night.

The thought of them reminds her of the Sea Sprite, who in some ways is rather waif-like. She also tends to scamper to the side like a crab, in her spirit. She avoids confrontation and being tied down to a commitment. It is hard to obtain a straight answer from her because she always looks at things from alternative points of view. As the mother knocks a pile of rotting, smelly seaweed with her foot, tiny sand-hoppers suddenly fire themselves high into the air.

Then the mother is mindful of female turtles, which climb onto the beach on a certain day of the year, at sunset. During the night, they labour to dig holes with their flippers, then lay their eggs in these holes. By dawn, they have buried their egg clutches and returned to the ocean. They seem to be very trusting of the nature of the coast. When the young turtles hatch out, at night, weeks later, they make a dash for the sea, on their tiny, sturdy legs. They already have great strength, sweeping through the sand, their sole focus honed for the sea.

The mother's thoughts return to the moment and the place where she is. She seems to stop breathing for a moment as she discovers a delicate, white shell, almost hidden against the white sand. At first, her eyes are only caught by its shadow.

She picks it up with care. It is too delicate to express. It resembles alabaster, but the colour is soft not shiny. It has long spikes projecting from it. It also has a papery mantle and a papery mane, projecting from different edges of its curve. They are all but transparent. As she turns it over, it feels light in her hand.

Indians believe that the blast of a conch shell will banish evil spirits, avert natural disasters and deter poisonous creatures. Does this delicate thing have the strength of character to offer such protection? Or is it safer to seek protection from Nereides, as the Sea Sprite has an affinity with them. A nereid is an ethereal creature that lives in the sea. She is a sea nymph.

Nereides dwell in the Aegean Sea, with their father Nereus, the Old Man of the Sea, in the depths, within a palace of gold. They symbolise everything that is beautiful, and kind about the sea. It is said that their melodious voices sing as they dance. They are graceful, barefoot young women, crowned with branches of red coral and dressed in white silk robes edged with gold.

The Nereides offer protection to those on the sea, coming to the aid of those in distress. Each one is connected to an aspect of the sea: salty brine, sea foam, sand, rocks, waves and currents as well as various skills of the sea. When they are not in their golden palace, they sometimes spend time in their silvery grotto, an alternative dwelling. Later, they run with small dolphins or fish in their hands. At other times, they ride on the backs of dolphins or seahorses.

While the mother is holding the precious shell, she begins to be aware of shells from other places. This shell in her hand must have a visionary quality. Some of the shells that she sees are pink and beige, like lingerie, others are shaped in the forms of scorpions or octopus. Some shells look like coral.

The shells are textured, smooth or shiny. Their sizes range from tiny to huge. Some have internal surfaces like mother-of pearl, including nautilus shells and abalone shells. The Sea Sprite would like these. Some others are precise in their form, while others again seem furry or jagged. Some shells are striped, others are patterned with lines of dots. Some are covered with African designs like dress material or modern art.

Shells

flowers of the sea
all shapes
all colours
textures

blossoming now
and will not fade

these shells
these flowers of the beach

The mother is amazed at how many different shells there are. There are shells in bright colours, others in pastels. Some are spiky and hairy, some are smooth inside, white or pink or green. Some could be mistaken for seaweed because they are dark brown and spiky. Some shells are very detailed in their surface designs: some look like embroidery, others are covered with blobs and dots.

Some shells have pointed cones, others have flat tops. Some are crinkled, like folded material, and some are dainty like paper. Some pagoda shells are shaped into the forms of fairy tale castles or palaces. The Sea Sprite would like these, too.

One shell seems to mimic a flower with its red lip, dotted with white. Other shells also look like flowers or candles. Some have delicate, parallel spines, others are frilled.

The Sea Sprite's mother, whose real name is Laura, puts the original white shell in her dripping pocket and the visions cease. She takes a few steps. She is familiar with some eastern religions, and her thoughts go there, now. One of the ones she knows is Buddhism, which says that the conch appears as an auspicious mark on a divinely endowed being. She takes a few more steps.

Then, for a moment, Laura stops again and stands still. She thinks about waves.

Waves of the sea represent constant change and movement, sometimes circular like the molecules of water in a wave, sometimes terminal like the crash of a wave, sometimes large like a tidal wave, or a storm surge, sometimes small like a ripple on the surface. The sea represents Chaos, the primordial potential, the original Mother from whom life emerged.

In the dream of the sea, the Sea Sprite plays in the surf. In the air, there is the salty smell of the ocean. Foam drips from her projections as well as crowning her head. She wears the water like a garment. Seaweed joins her in the fun, as she lets some of the waves break against her body. They nearly knock her over. At other times, she catches the wave before it breaks, and rides it like a billowing balloon in to shore. She arrives, deposited on her chest on the silken sand.

On the shore, there are pebbles, made smoothly round by the continual washing of the waves. She crawls over so she can see them better. Some of the pebbles are green or brown, and some of them are black. The black ones are shiny when wet by seawater and they seem to have depth. The Sea Sprite thinks she can almost catch a glimpse of her face deep within them.

What she sees is reminiscent of a female spirit of the sea. It looks like a nereid.

Now, standing up, the Sea Sprite notices that golden-brown sprays and garlands of seaweed, decorated with brown berries, are strewn around on the beach, as well as sponges and pieces of white 'cuttlefish'. Tiny crabs make patterns on the crisp sand. Leaving their holes, they roll sand into little balls, which they spread out into shapes that resemble butterflies or even mandalas.

There are also shells on the beach. Some of them are pink and shaped like fans. Some of them are pointed, spiralling inward to secret places. The Sea Sprite holds spirals in high regard. To her, they represent the spiritual journey, which always moves forward, is always similar to what went before but always a little different.

Some of the shells on the beach are from abalone, full of graceful curves. Inside them, the blended pinks and blues and whites reflect the fluid, milky soul of the Sea Sprite. Silhouettes of tall rocks are reflected in shallow water and wet sand.

Then, leaving the dream for a moment, Laura, the Sea Sprite's mother, stops again to stand still. She listens.

At first, she can't hear anything, except the *shoosh* of the waves on the beach and the cry of the seagulls. Then she hears it – a soft murmuring in between breaking waves. It is coming from the rock pool around the corner of the headland. Laura makes her way in that direction. Her journey begins as she moves from one part of the sea, one part of the coast, to another.

Rocky Coast

Laura steps from one rock to another. Then, she gazes into a rock-pool filled with moving water.

when waves
break against rocks
and sea water surging
meets and washes

and is frantic
not relenting

it threatens
and calls

and absorbs

it shows us
our depths

drowning us with
vulnerabilities

self-pity
and tender exposures

control dissolves
self is swept away
and framework lost

Laura looks away again, well-nigh at once. She can't face this, she doesn't want to know.

She walks on until she comes to a different place. These rugged rocks have steep sides where they meet the water, so that waves hit them with great force. There is accompanying noise and spectacular splashes as spray fans out with violence.

This activity of the maternal sea reminds her of a painful event that occurred years ago, with her own mother. It was a tipping point in her life, as if she nearly drowned.

At that time, Laura had just begun to enjoy poetry. Poetry gave her life. It was like water to a flower. The only time Laura felt alive and powerful was to do with poetry. It not only expressed her very being, it also showed her who she was.

She belonged to a poetry circle, where both reading and writing poetry were encouraged. The members would meet on a regular basis and read their own work to each other. They often expressed very deep parts of themselves. They were bringing out the subtle half-conscious side into the outside world.

Partnering each other, to workshop their writing, was emphasised and valued. The partners would usually come to know each other well, often discussing the content of the poems at length, as well as their form. In this way, they shared many personal and significant aspects of their lives.

Laura's mother was conservative and didn't like change. She didn't modify her speech or her clothes as time went by. She loved to look back on the past, taking her standards from there. If the rest of the world changed around her, she narrowed her circle of acquaintances. She only spent time with people who were on a par with her.

She also undertook her role as a mother with great seriousness. She didn't have a sense of humour, anyway. She saw it as vital that she instructed her daughter in detail in all the things she needed to know. These included everything from sewing to fashion to politics to manners to studying for exams. The most important lessons were morals.

Her religion was important to her. She wanted her own life to be perfect, so that it would be shining and reaching high. It was as if she wanted to view the world from a point in the sky. These aspirations caused a lot of tension in her life. Sometimes, Laura felt she had to hold her breath so as not to destroy the illusion of romantic perfection.

As well as having these high ideals, Laura's mother was busy cooking and cleaning. She did the washing in a copper, stirring it with a stick, then squeezing it through a mangle. Once, she caught her hand in the mangle, splitting her flesh and shearing it. She polished the kitchen floor on a regular basis, and every few months, on her hands and knees, she scraped the layers of polish off, as it had turned yellow. Then she started again.

She cooked a different meal each night of the week, each time providing a hot dessert to go with it. Sunday roast lamb with three or four vegetables was a highlight, with home-made mint sauce. Table manners and etiquette were enforced. She also preserved fruit and baked cakes, arranging flowers from her own garden. She had brown thumbs from all her gardening. On Sunday mornings, she donned her hat and gloves, and checked that the seams in her stockings were straight, before going to church.

Laura's mother was intense, always walking fast and working hard. This was her way to deal with emotions. Sometimes her view of the world expanded so much that she lost touch with reality. She kept on extrapolating about things until what she was saying became absurd.

Her moral sense was tied in with the importance of her religion. This religion forbad any artistic endeavours. They were not only seen as a waste of time but were perceived as frivolous. They were also thought of as indulgent in addition to encouraging loss of self-control.

Poetry was regarded as most improper, because it was thought to involve delusion as well as trickery. There was a play on words that bent your mind. Hating poetry, she projected all her own negativity onto those who indulged in it. Sometimes, she even lost her temper, but she never hurt anyone.

One night, Laura came home late. She was confused and on edge, her body quite tense, because her poetry partner had come with her. He seemed not to know the unwritten rule that there was no poetry in her house, nor any reminder of it. Laura felt the ground give way beneath her.

She didn't know what to do. She couldn't send him away, because he wouldn't understand. It was forbidden to spell out the nature of the taboo, so she couldn't explain the situation to him. She was not good at conversation, anyway. She felt mute.

She had to remove him from that place. She had to phone a taxi to take him away.

She went inside but discovered that the phone had been moved to her mother's bedroom. She knew that was bad. She drew in her breath. Why didn't she go back outside to seek a solution? Did she make the mistake of trusting her mother?

After some deliberation, she walked into that lion's den with great courage as well as bravado. She held her head high. She thought she could take the phone without waking her mother, but her mother woke up at once.

"What are you doing?" she said.

"Just collecting the phone… to ring a taxi… to take him home."

"What time is it?" It was 5:00 a.m.

"What are you doing, coming home so late? What have you been doing? Have you been with poets?"

"You are just so moralistic." The words blew over her mother like a metal rope of dangerous energy.

Her mother threw back the blankets with force.

"It would be a good thing if you were more moral," she said. "Where is he now?"

"Outside, waiting."

Laura's mother leapt out of bed and rushed down the passage.

"Where is the carving-knife?"

Laura raced to the front door, and went outside in a great panic, to warn him to go away. She told him to escape, to go like a rocket, to run. Her mother had a knife.

However, she didn't take the knife, after all. Laura's terror had tweaked something in her mother to make her realise what she was doing.

Then she had to justify her actions. She had to explain to Laura why she had done it.

She disguised it in the form of preaching. In her nightie and bare feet, she half stood, half knelt, on the arm of an armchair, so that she was looking down on Laura. She set out to tell Laura why poetry was wrong. It seemed like the greatest possible evil, that Laura was the greatest possible wrong-doer, that she was worthless.

The one thing that made Laura feel alive was wrong. Her very being was wrong and shouldn't exist.

Mother Sea

mother sea rejected me
did not wash me in to shore
did not cast me away
with seaweed and shells
she threw me with storm fury
against jags and points and blades
lashed me repeatedly
picking me up
and throwing me onto knife points

shreds and tears became food
for the teeth of sharks
already masticated
my central self was gone
threads of garment scattered

in deeps under waves
sinking without form
under weight of water
fading

After two hours of destruction, Laura had two hours of sleep.

When she awoke and arose, she felt like an automaton, stiff in the mind, grey and thin. Her mind had been beaten until there was no will left, no will at all, except for a faint desire to escape.

She tried on the idea of boarding an interstate train. She thought of killing herself. She collected some razor blades, putting them in her handbag.

She left the house and walked and walked. At the end of the road, she turned and went up the hill. She found a paddock on the hillside with a few eucalypts as well as scraggy shrubs.

Laura sat down at the base of a tree. She prayed. She recited the Lord's Prayer three times.

Then she took out a razor blade, and cut the inside of both wrists, and waited to die…

Although she didn't die, the feeling that motivated her attempted suicide, stayed with her. It was in the form of a brown cloud that enveloped her.

For much of the rest of her life, visitations of the cloud came every now and then. Until one day, after many years, the brown cloud gained strength. Brown was all she knew, making her body stiff and slow. Stuck.

Now, Laura observes a seal playing in the deep water. There is delight here after all. However, she walks over the rocks to reach a calmer place, further inland. Then she becomes enthralled by the life in the rock pools.

Some free seaweed floats, while other seaweed is attached to the rocks by its holdfast. Some green and brown weed is like long hair, waving, roughened by the water. Laura notices the variations between other kinds of weed. Olive coloured seaweed is delicate and leafy. Red coloured weed is redolent, in its shape, of a posy of small flowers. Some green seaweed is shaped like blunt twigs, while other pieces look like frilly petticoats.

Because of the force of the waves on the rocks, most of all when the tide is in, animals living here need to have a good grip on the rock. This is exactly how Laura feels. She needs to cling to a firm foundation within herself, not letting go, for fear of her memories.

Animals achieve this grip in various ways. When the tide is in, limpets feed on algae (seaweed) growing on the rocks. They hold onto the rocks against the waves, each with a single, muscular foot.

Between waves, as well as when the tide is out, they pull themselves hard against the rock, making a watertight seal. In so doing, they make a groove on the rock, which is a mirror image of their shell. By following their own trail of slime, they can return to the same place every time they leave it. Laura wonders whether this describes some people.

Barnacles use a kind of "cement" to fasten themselves to a rock. They stay in the same place for their whole life. This defines some people, such as Laura's own mother.

Tough threads connect mussels to rock. These animals create a sticky liquid which becomes solid when it touches water. When the tide is out, mussels tighten their paired shells.

Nevertheless, some birds can still eat them. As Laura watches, an oystercatcher hammers away at mussel shells with its powerful bill, trying to smash them. When it finds one it can't smash, it uses its bill to lever the shell open.

Absent-mindedly, Laura massages her new shell in her pocket. She knows she isn't looking at a pale green flower when she spies a sea anemone. It is, in fact, an animal. It uses its long, stinging tentacles to catch its prey by impaling it on many microscopic poison darts so that the prey is paralysed. Then, the anemone wraps its tentacles around the prey, drawing it into its mouth, in the centre of its body. Toxic hugs like these are given only by the worst of people.

At low tide, sea anemones pull their tentacles into the base of their bodies, to conserve water; however, they always stay glued to the same spot.

Shore crabs, as well as hermit crabs, cling onto the rocks with their jointed legs. Even some fish can hold on. Laura's shell tells her about the two-spotted clingfish. With its two pelvic fins, it forms a sucker disc on its belly. It uses this disc to stick itself to the rock. Some people cling to other people like this.

Chitons are other animals that fasten to rocks. Several different plates make up their shells. The Sea Sprite also forms strong attachments.

At night, octopus hunt crabs and fish in rock pools. No matter what their size, they can squeeze through the smallest cracks in the rock. Not many people can do this, but in an argument, the Sea Sprite squeezes through any cracks that are left open. She can see to the heart of the matter in a few seconds, seizing her advantage.

Observing wildlife always lifts Laura's spirits. In the shallow rock pools, long-legged wading birds such as grey herons, white egret, and black and white avocet, as well as sea gulls and black-capped terns, can be seen.

Above the waterline, seals sometimes come to nurse their young or to rest. Laura likes to rest on the rocks, in the sun, as well, even when she's not tired. The rocks transmit their warmth to her body, easing any aches. She can forget her troubling past for a few moments.

Laura's curiosity stimulates her to keep rubbing her shell. There are large numbers of wading birds here above the water line. Besides oystercatchers, which eat limpets and mussels, there are turnstones, which flip over pebbles and seaweed to find their food, and black cormorants, which stand in the sun, with their wings outstretched to dry their feathers. All the cliff-dwelling birds congregate in large numbers, taking several trips out to sea each day.

Then, as Laura, the Sea Sprite's mother, gazes around at these birds, and then downwards, she sees her daughter, at last. At the same moment, she is aware of a teardrop full of the ocean. Her daughter, the Sea Sprite, is lying on a rock like a mermaid, crying herself to sleep.

Her mother walks over and caresses her, stroking her soft temples where her curls wisp. She cups the Sea Sprite's head in her other hand. With a sense of reassurance along with safety, she gathers the Sea Sprite in her arms, making her way out of the rock pools. The journey continues as they make their way from one part of the coast to another.

The Beach

The mother puts down the Sea Sprite and they move on, both walking, over smooth pebbles, which squeak and crack under foot. As they continue, they reach the sandy beach, where they keep walking until they find a sand dune to lean against.

Now, brooding clouds are defeated by glimmers of light. Illumination wakens the sky.

Waves overlap and crescent on the beach. A shiver ripples, as the green and blue edges of water meet the sand, making a white, lacy pattern. Wind kisses the water, many pleats of sea concertina. Then, bubbles phosphoresce as waves start to form.

The two women sit down, then the Sea Sprite puts her head in her mother's lap. They are not really mother and daughter: they are lovers, but they feel like mother and daughter. The Sea Sprite is frail.

She is more of a wraith
than a person
as if
if one turned away

for an instant
she would slip between pages
and disappear

Her mother, Laura, cares for her.

Their love is full of affection.

petals rain softly
like the love between women

When the Sea Sprite kisses Laura, it is as if she donates a poem to her mouth. Now, the two of them are happy just to be together, softly touching.

As Laura looks around her, she smiles to think of the primitive-looking horseshoe crabs which come in thousands to spawn as well as to lay their eggs near the high tide line. Weeks later, the larvae climb up through the sand grains, swimming out on the receding high tide.

Pristine white seagulls fly overhead, going '*caw*' as they land. They keep the beach clean.

Shells surprise Laura again and again, as she fondles her own shell. Some are knobbly, some are like sand. Some have radiating spikes like a child's picture of the sun, some have slender towers like minarets.

A few spikes are long, some are short. Some are in the same colour as the rest of the shell, others are in contrasting colours. Some shells look naked, some have flowing effects. One looks like a wedding-cake at a commitment ceremony between two women.

All these effects are found in twisting cowrie shells. The same ones are repeated in flatter bi-valve shells.

Spiral Shells

spiral shapes
seeking
inner
still point

returning
bringing peace
as gift
for the world

Then, the Sea Sprite begins to cry. It is about something which happened some time ago, on land. She was violated by a man.

She was stunned when it happened. She couldn't take it all in. It did not occur to her that it was rape. It was not in a back alley, he was not roughly dressed or unshaven. He did not have a knife. He had been introduced to her by people she knew.

Afterwards, the Sea Sprite felt she had lost all sense of control over her body. Her brain was numb. She was lost, wandering in a maze of nebulous cloud tunnels. Her will was broken. While she couldn't move at times, she lost all motivation for living. This went on for many years.

Did he go on to success in life? People thought she was a failure: they never knew the reason why.

The mother, Laura, holds the Sea Sprite with gentleness, brushing the loose hair away from her face and rubbing her back. What more can she do? She can never take away this pain. The Sea Sprite cries often.

The mother rocks the Sea Sprite in her arms until she goes to sleep. They stay in the same place for some time. Then rising, they start to walk.

Estuary

Leaving the beach, the Sea Sprite's mother, Laura, and the Sea Sprite climb through the soft sand of the dunes, the marram grass and low shrubs. On the way down, their feet break up the crisp surface of the sand.

Laura recalls the names of the plants. At first, the vegetation includes spinifex grass, the bright colours of the pigface succulent, the pinkish-mauve flowers of the vine goatsfoot, and yellow guinea flower.

As they walk further, coastal sheoaks take over with their hanging, needle-like leaves. Finally, they come to a woodland of tall shrubs with yellow bottle-brushes. These are banksias.

The path to the estuary emerges out of the woodland. The women walk on. The Sea Sprite is feeling better now, for the moment. She would like to know whether they are going to see any crabs. Laura shrugs her shoulders, smiling.

As they arrive at the water, they pass feathery reeds, and in other places, the large brown cylindrical tops of bulrushes. Then again, there are shorter rushes as well as sedges, with knobbly flowers, close to the bank. The Sea Sprite wishes she could paint some of the scenes here. The interest lies in the contrasting textures. Laura promises to bring her here again with some paints.

The reeds and the bulrushes spread out into the water channel, cleansing the water and providing habitat for many small creatures, as Laura learnt in biology. These range from microscopic organisms to fish seeking food as well as shelter. Snails crawl along the lower stalks of the plants, feeding on algae and rubbish. Laura is excited by the diversity of life all in one place. She can feel her heart beating fast. She is awake all over.

Then she sees a large, white pelican floating in a clear patch of water, watching her and the Sea Sprite. Laura and the pelican stare into each other's eye.

She muses on the fecundity of this place, where fresh water from the river exists with salt water. The high tide brings up brine, which falls below the freshwater in the same way that Laura's subconscious drops below her conscious mind. Doris is the nereid in charge of the mixing of fresh water with salt and Laura can feel her presence. In the estuary, these wedges of different kinds of water eventually mingle. However, before this happens, the opposing flows slow the river water, which drops its load of sediment. This fertile ooze supports a huge abundance of life.

Laura is not the only one to be grateful for the presence of the nereid. Giving Laura a big smile, the Sea Sprite is also pleased. Rubbing her shell, Laura becomes aware that the numbers of species here are almost doubled, because both fresh and saltwater species exist in the same place.

This is a subliminal zone, beyond conscious awareness, because it is hard to grasp. It is neither river nor sea, neither land nor water. Sunlight slants off the surface of the water, so that it shines and sparkles. Laura's heart stretches, opening in her chest, in response to the shining light.

The level of water in the estuary ebbs and flows with the tide, as do feelings in Laura and the Sea Sprite, as well as feelings between them. They feel very close, in an unspoken way.

Limnoreia is the nereid in charge of salt marshes. It is because of her that most of the vegetation in the estuary proper, lower down, between the water channels, is samphire, pink and succulent. It survives by excreting salt. There are large and small islands of mud, channels and bays of water.

This is an insubstantial place where one cannot find a firm foothold, and it is always changing. It is like the Sea Sprite, who is a

spectral naiad
water nymph
of sparkling light
hidden between
layers of physicality

On the one hand, the women know Nereides, which are sea nymphs. On the other hand, naiads are freshwater nymphs. The type of naiad that lives in marshes like this estuary, is the Eleionomae, the mother, Laura, discovers as she touches the shell. She and the Sea Sprite had better be careful, as these naiads are known to create illusions and lead travellers astray. They can be quite dangerous.

Mists over the waters here create an effect that suggests illusions. The mists come and go and move upwards in shreds and are somewhat opaque, so they are hard to see through. It is fortunate that the women have the shell to guide them.

The estuary is a dynamic environment that changes a great deal, depending on the tide. When the tide is in, bivalve molluscs extend their siphons up through the muddy sediment. This is a metaphor for life. Laura needs to rise above everything that's depressing or muddy: she needs a siphon, or a spiritual lifeline. The creatures sieve the water for plankton.

As well as this, lugworms eat the mud itself, digesting the organic matter and expelling the rest. This is what depression feels like: muddy on the outside and the inside. Predatory pink ragworms stick their heads out of their burrows to grab shrimps.

Feeding on all these invertebrates, several species of fish, namely drums, croakers and grunts, communicate by sound. They liven up the translucent peace of the surrounds.

Marine fish in the estuary include grey mullet as well as peacock flounder. Laura caresses the shell in her pocket. It has a universal view, not restricted to one geographic place. To complete the food chain, sinuous river otters from the north, and pelicans, black and white ibis, and herons from the south, all hunt for fish together here. The Sea Sprite would like to paint the birds as well, especially their different shapes.

When the tide falls, mud flats are exposed so they are seen to be teeming with life. Laura makes the mistake of trying to walk across the flats, but mud oozes up between her toes as well as around the sides of her feet. The mud holds her feet, sucking her in. She is frightened that she will end up even deeper inside the mud.

Mud is something she is cautious of, because it reminds her of the muddy feelings that sometimes obscure her awareness. For them to suck her in, for them to overwhelm her, would be the worst thing she could imagine. Mud weighs her down, even making it hard to move.

However, while she is lost in thought, her feet are becoming more entrenched in the mud. In her fraught efforts to free herself, she loses balance and falls over. Was this the work of the naiad? She lands on the pocket which contains her special shell. It digs into her leg, taking her back in time.

She remembers being a seven-year-old. Her mother was brushing her hair. Despite being a perfectionist when it came to her house, Laura's mother had a rather dowdy personal appearance. She was short as well as fat, shaped rather like a French loaf of bread, with a small sphere on top of a larger sphere. A belt held her waist in.

She had been a widow for several years but wasn't looking for anyone else. She had let herself go. Her clothes were dictated by her religion: plain and simple. Nothing should distract attention from God. She wore old fashioned clothes, which were often second-hand, and support stockings with lace-up shoes. Her hair was straight and black and short and stuck out over her ears. She didn't wear make-up and her glasses were utilitarian.

She brushed Laura's hair into a style that Laura didn't like but had to tolerate. Then her mother pulled out a second-hand jumper which was grey. Laura hated grey. Her mother insisted, only stopping to suck her false teeth back into place. Laura put on the jumper. She felt a pinch in her heart.

Her mother always cut her off with her loud voice, before Laura had a chance to speak. Laura was too frightened of her mother to ask for a new pair of shoes, even though her current ones were uncomfortable because they didn't fit. She knew this fear wasn't good.

Laura's mother was brash. If she could not do the right thing, she would go ahead and do the wrong thing in an obvious way. One day, she bent over to pull up her underpants while Laura sat behind her. Laura had a view of a black bush of hair which was ugly. How could her mother do that to her? How could she transmit such ugliness? Laura wanted to retch. In addition, she knew she wasn't supposed to see it. She was overpowered with anger.

Laura had no place to respond to any of the events like these. If she questioned her mother, Laura lost the argument. So, she stopped trying. Not only could she not love this woman who seemed to dwell in dark shadows, but the distorted little green shoots in her heart had been cut.

So, even before she grew up to discover poetry, Laura did not like her mother. The clash about poetry later in her life was inevitable.

Now, Laura thinks. She doesn't want to be a mother, if it means being like her own mother. She finds that thought repugnant. What a horrible woman. Laura would like to remove herself from the very thought of her mother. No longer does she want to be a mother, in any way, even to the Sea Sprite. Laura doesn't want any evocation of ugliness. She would prefer a relationship of equals, a relationship where each of them stands on their own two feet. She must tell the Sea Sprite. She needs to discuss this with her.

Here in the estuary, Laura manages to stand up by leaning forward, but her legs go deeper into the mud. She needs to hold onto some overhanging vegetation, a River Red Gum branch, with the help of the nereid, Limnoreia, so that she can lever herself free of the mud.

The Sea Sprite puts her hand on Laura's back, transmitting a meditative calm to her. Laura is warm and tingly and relaxed. Being loved like this makes her confident again, so she tells the Sea Sprite about her experience and her decision. The Sea Sprite wants to wait to discuss it until there is somewhere for them to sit down. Laura takes a deep breath then puts this matter aside. She continues to look around her.

Crabs are scurrying about on the mud, which pleases the Sea Sprite, while birds are feeding on small creatures within the mud. There are levels of mud suitable for birds with all various kinds of beaks. The longest bills go deepest but short bills seek food in the shallower levels.

Many birds are present, in flocks, or pairs or as individuals. As Laura rubs her fingers along the conch shell, her perception opens to creatures from the wide world who are all present in this place of fantasy. She becomes aware of an enormous crowd of pink flamingos from Africa, over to her left. The flock is seething. All the birds are moving a little as they feed. Their long legs lift them above the mud, but their curving necks reach down. Different shades of pink on their feathers as well as on their skin give texture to the mass.

Over to her right, amongst the reflections of light on the wet surface of the mud, there are smaller birds. These include masked plovers with their yellow face masks, black-capped terns, glossy ibis with rainbow-coloured plumage and white egrets. The Sea Sprite is interested again, because of the range of different colours presented by the birds.

This place, this estuary, seems to exist in the subconscious, because it is transitional and beyond the polarities of land versus water. It is at once brackish, muddy and oozing, yet at the same time, shining and crystalline. The light glints, so that Laura can only see the sparkle out of the corner of her eye.

The glitter on the surface of the shallow water makes Laura think of the Sea Sprite. Crystal light shines from her edges where her soft curls overlap. In this in-between place, the loving, delicate intuition of the Sea Sprite is prevalent. Laura realises that this soft, fluid stillness is always there, underneath, but here it is more present in the awareness.

Together, Laura and the Sea Sprite walk around the estuary until they come to the mouth of the river. The river bends around, first one way and then the other, whereupon it comes out between ochre-coloured cliffs, to the sea. A funnel of sea tickles the corner of a cliff. Green water effervesces against the cliff contours. Like the sea, the cliffs bubble and tumble in turmoil, writhing and twisting, but frozen.

In these cliffs, there are small caves, at an upper level, which are full of pigeons, moving in and out. The cooing of the birds reaches the women on the shore.

At the water's edge, in the shallow waves, stand two birds, side by side, looking out to sea. One is a silver gull, the other a white egret. The latter is a little taller than the gull, but it is obvious to Laura and the Sea Sprite that they are there together. They are friends. They have stood like this, together, on the beach, at the water's edge, on many occasions. Egrets inhabit the estuary as a norm, but in this case, one has extended its range a little, past the mouth of the river onto the beach where the salt water washes.

Mangroves

Carrying the Sea Sprite, the Sea Sprite's mother, Laura, rounds the headland, coming upon a bay, which includes a tangled forest of mangroves. There are red mangroves, apple mangroves and a few coconut palms, as well as tropical rainforest trees. The mangroves have circular, light green leaves, which excrete salt. The leaves of the other trees are dark green.

Walking on the beach, between mangrove roots, is cumbersome. The roots are like stilts in the air, sometimes bunched together in triangular shapes, like struts for tiny wigwams. They absorb air for the plants, as most of their roots are under water. Trying to avoid the aerial roots means that Laura can't establish a rhythm with her feet. She keeps being interrupted. This means that she nearly drops the Sea Sprite every time she clambers over a jutting out root.

There is not much beach here anyway, as the mangroves come down almost to the water's edge, so she walks behind and between them. The sand is flat and shining wet, hinting at something away, away.

As Laura touches the shell in her pocket, she becomes aware of proboscis monkeys with their big noses and the ruffs around their necks, in the trees, eating the salty mangrove leaves. She imagines mud lobsters out at night with burrowing crabs eating fallen leaves.

Mud lobsters eat tiny pieces of organic matter in the mud and sand. To obtain enough nutrition, they need to process large amounts of these materials. Huge mounds are left outside their burrows, some reaching three metres high. Laura gives a wry smile as she doesn't like mud, but she can see that the mud lobster rejoices in it.

In the mangroves, there are also sky-blue fiddler crabs, each with one enormous claw, fighting off rivals for mates. Laura can visualise Sea Sprite fighting off rivals for her. Her fighting wouldn't stick to the rules, but it would be most effective.

As tiny creatures buzz, sea snakes come in on high tides with terrestrial snakes also visiting. Pythons are attracted by large numbers of flying-foxes. Laura has a fascination for snakes of all kinds.

Further up the beach, at the water's edge, is a prehistoric-looking monster – a salt-water crocodile. Drops of water falling from its long chin catch the light as it climbs out of the water. It has a corrugated line all the way down its curving spine and four stubby legs, and it is the largest living reptile. Its teeth, which can be seen at the sides of its mouth, are longer than the width of Laura's arm.

The Sea Sprite screams and wriggles in Laura's arms. Laura cannot hold her, so she falls to the ground. In her confusion, the Sea Sprite runs towards the crocodile, so that Laura spins and runs, stretching out her arms towards her. She manages to grab the child's wrist, hoisting her up, away from harm. She shakes the child onto her hip then clasps her to her chest. The Sea Sprite is still screaming.

Laura walks away from the crocodile. Gradually, the screaming dies down, becoming sobs, then hiccups. Laura's back aches as she wishes for more adult company, more equal sharing of responsibility, fewer crises.

After some time, they come upon a kayak left on the beach. As it seems to be deserted, yet quite intact, Laura decides to take it out onto the ocean. She puts down her child then tries to lift the kayak to carry it to the water. She finds it heavy as well as awkward. It is hard to balance without either the front or the back tipping too far.

Once they reach the sea, Laura stands up to her thighs in water, while the kayak bounces on top. She manages to lift the Sea Sprite in first then Laura attempts to enter the boat behind her. How can she prevent the boat from tipping over while she does this? There is nothing to hold onto. She scissors her legs while she jumps, so that one-foot lands in the kayak before the other. She sits down, exhausted, yet exhilarated by her ingenuity in putting them both safely in the vessel.

There are a few small waves. Laura picks up the paddle. She dips the blade into the water on the right side of the boat. She turns the paddle as she changes from right to the left side of the boat. There are marks on top of the right paddle blade, so that she knows she has the paddle the right way around. She grips it with her right hand, while her left hand is looser, so that the handle can rotate in her hand.

Little by little, the kayak moves, in a diagonal line, out to sea yet along the beach, against the current. Laura's legs begin to ache, so she bends them, trying to rest her feet in the hollows in the kayak. This doesn't work, so Laura cries out in pain. Then she leans back a little, hunching her shoulders, trying to hold onto the uneven surface of the sides of the boat. This is uncomfortable but stops her legs from aching.

However, she cannot paddle in this position, so she keeps moving, changing around, then back again. The Sea Sprite leans back so she is lying down, with her head close to Laura's lap. This is relaxed and indulgent. She can gaze at the sky, seeming quite wistful. She talks about poetry, then the way light plays on the water. Drops of water fall into her eyes and onto her face from the blades of the paddle as they alternate up then down in her peripheral vision.

In her adult voice, she says she likes poetry, because you need to search for exactly the right word to express what you mean. Then Laura says she likes it, moreover, because you can find new ways to create the language. They think they hear Nereides, laughing and playing in the distance.

Laura moves again, trying to find a comfortable position to ease her aching legs. Her arms are tired from paddling.

The water is grey and opaque, so no wildlife can be seen, no turtles or fish or sharks or whales, only an occasional booby, with its bright blue feet tucked up out of the way for flying, or a frigate bird, with no sign of its large, inflatable, red pouch. However, one small white fish leaps out of the water. It is trying to escape the larger fish that is chasing it.

In her pocket, Laura feels her shell which tells her there are over 70 species of fish that visit the mangroves at some stage in their life cycle. However, the mudskipper is the only fish to live here throughout its entire lifespan. Barramundi and Mangrove Jack are two fish that breed in the mangroves.

The Sea Sprite daydreams that she is floating. She is aware of being safe, knowing the rainforest is there, as well as the smooth white beach. Laura observes that, from the sea, the rainforest seems to be shimmering. A sense of beauty fills them both.

The water is choppy close to the next headland, so Laura turns the boat around so that they can explore the place where the mangroves come right down into the sea. By touching the conch shell, Laura can see a stout, grey night heron sitting on the prop roots of the mangroves, contrary to its normal nocturnal habits, as well as a brightly-coloured kingfisher waiting on a branch. Both these birds are gazing intently into the water. Quickly, without warning, each one attacks a separate underwater fish.

The shell tells Laura that there are 230 species of birds to be seen here, most of whom are visitors. Two of these are the beach stone curlew, with its long legs and long beak, as well as the lesser noddy, which builds its nest in the tree branches.

The boat moves in close to the stilted mangroves, behind a few of the outer stilts. The light green foliage of the mangroves hangs over the roots. This water is a nursery for fish, and many young fish live amongst the roots.

Laura's shell tells her that many snails live here, eating microscopic plants. The mangrove oyster colonises trunks and aerial roots, in large colonies. The tree-boring beetle is light green with a pink patch on its back. The false water rat is rare, but the common water rat nests near the mangroves. Illidge's ant-blue butterfly can be seen resting on a mangrove orchid.

Wavy light falls through the leaves, penetrating the water and showing up the underwater roots. Some roots come up from the water, seeking air. Bursts of light on the water are striped like ripples.

The boat goes over the top of some horizontal roots that are only just submerged. The bottom of the boat touches them, then the boat stops moving.

Laura swears. She uses her paddle to poke and prod and push the roots and branches until the boat is free.

Now that the boat is moving again, Laura paddles with the current, back along the beach. The surface of the ocean is full of ripples as well as curves and mini waves, as if it is a moving sculpture. As the boat continues, the waves become larger.

Laura turns the kayak so that it is pointed towards the beach and is at right angles to the waves. As a bigger wave comes, she paddles hard to catch it. It lifts them up, carrying them towards the shore. Laura and the Sea Sprite are buoyant. They feel in tune with the wave. They repeat the process. The kayak surfing sometimes carries them 30 metres so that they end up right in on the sand. They keep doing it over and over, until they are at one with the wave.

kayak surfing
is like upbeat floating
lifting one up
over cacophony
of awkwardness
and fear

As the day progresses, the Sea Sprite becomes tired, and starts to wriggle. She stands up in the boat. This causes the kayak to change direction so that it is parallel to the breaking wave. It also tips at an angle so that it curves into the underside of the surge. Laura is tipped out of the boat, landing on her bottom in half a metre of sea water. The water is quite warm, and she has no trouble finding her footing. She stands up, her clothes heavy with water. Her hair is the only thing not wet.

Laura catches her breath, and the two of them laugh about it. However, Laura wishes that her companion could be more considerate.

They dragged the boat up onto the sand, and placed the paddles in it. Laura's clothes cling to her, water streaming down her legs. With time, her dress starts to dry in the light wind as the women walk along the beach.

Once Laura's dress is dry, the two women sit down on the sand. Laura wants to talk about the decision she made after falling in the mud, in the estuary. They talk. They talk and talk, but they don't communicate. The Sea Sprite occupies herself with making witty replies to what Laura is saying. She keeps going off on tangents. Then, at last, she says she'll do what Laura wants, that is, attempt to grow up. She will also try to be more independent. These tasks turn out to be more difficult than she expects.

However, Laura is pleased. She suggests that they continue their journey to visit every aspect of the ocean, as this will help them develop. To improve their relationship, they will both have to grow. They have already been in the surf, on the sandy and pebbly beaches, on the rocks, in the sand dunes, in the estuary, under the cliffs, as well as in the mangroves. The next parts of their travels will be underwater.

Coastal Waters
Kelp Forests

After Laura and the Sea Sprite leave the mangrove beach, they walk back around the headland. As they enter the original sandy shore, the sun is starting to set. There are streaks of pale pink across the sky.

They walk past the mouth of the river and past the place where the egret and the gull are still standing gazing out to sea. The two women then turn, hold hands, and watch the sun setting into the sea. They observe its reflection like a column all the way to where they are. It seems to be calling to them, providing them with a pathway.

Just as the last curve of the sun's disk drops below the horizon, the two women start walking forward. After a few steps, the Sea Sprite stumbles, so Laura picks her up, carrying her until the water becomes deeper.

Laura experiences the water on her legs, then her abdomen. She walks up to the breaking waves, then keeps going. The water wets their bodies until only Laura's head is left dry. More of the Sea Sprite is still watertight because Laura is holding her up. Then Laura lets the Sea Sprite slip down her body so that she can tread water. Two heads are left.

Then they both jump up, still holding hands. They lift their bottoms up, and turn over, diving into the water, diving into the realm of the subconscious.

Laura's shell provides daylight for them, wherever they are. So, they can see that under the surface, the water looks a pale aqua colour, not dark blue as it does from outside. There are bubbles everywhere, ripples of light, then down below, the sand.

The sea is a dream and in dreams all things are possible. This means that Laura and Daphne don't have to worry about breathing under water, or any of the other practicalities of daily life. Dreams are concerned with more important matters.

The Sea Sprite's real name is Daphne, and now both she and Laura swim out deeper. These coastal waters are some of the richest waters in the sea. The river brings a stream of nutrients from land, while currents which up well bring organic matter and minerals from the deep. The waters are shallow over the continental shelf until this abruptly ends.

Closest to shore are the most fertile waters because light can penetrate to the full extent. Plants such as eelgrass, and algae, such as kelp and other seaweeds, provide habitat for huge numbers of creatures. The plentiful nutrients feed large clouds of phytoplankton (tiny plants), which are food for zooplankton (tiny animals). Fish eat them, then in turn, they provide food for seabirds.

Kelp are tall algae with leaves, that form dense forests. Sometimes, light shines through a break in the foliage. Pink and white sea slugs called nudibranchs, can be seen, with many vertical pink tubes on their backs. In some lights, despite being slugs, they look ethereal.

Kelp, being giant seaweed, needs holdfasts to anchor it to the rocks. These holdfasts look like the roots of plants, but they don't have the same structure or overall function. A grey seal lies on some kelp fronds and is lit up by patches of light.

Laura keeps stroking her shell, which tells her that the vertical kelp stems are tough and from them, grow strap-like fronds. These fronds extend a long way, sometimes even approaching 60m. Large air-filled bladders hold the kelp upright, so that it can find light for photosynthesis. At low tide, the kelp is exposed to air, but it never becomes desiccated, because it contains large amounts of algin. Algin retains water.

The feelings of Laura and Daphne become intertwined and tangled like the kelp, with occasional, lit up moments between the fronds. The more time they spend together, the less they can perceive each other with accuracy.

Laura becomes stressed from dealing with Daphne, carrying her on her back while continuing to swim, despite Daphne's tantrums. Laura's tense state makes her body ache. Daphne may squeal and scream but Laura doesn't know why. She asks Daphne what is wrong and what does she want, but Daphne just keeps on shrieking and screeching. The pressure to decide makes her worse.

Laura never does find out what is wrong with Daphne, at times like this. Perhaps just a generalised state of anxiety, which make her sensitive to everything.

Laura makes all the judgements and carries all the emotion. This responsibility exhausts her, so she, like the seal, lies down on the kelp fronds and massages her shell. This is restful because she feels as if she is part of the ecology of the kelp forest. She would like to surrender. However, when she remembers her relationship with Daphne, she wants change.

Many animals live on or among the kelp fronds. These range from sea snails, in their spiral shells, which can be tiny, to seals, which can be huge. The sea snails use their rasp-like tongues to scrape away at the fronds, while isopods (tiny crustaceans) munch the fronds. These small creatures are eaten by fish such as the large, brown kelp bass and bright orange Garibaldi. In turn, these fish are eaten by diving birds, sea lions and seals.

Laura and Daphne sit close together with their heads touching. Laura's hand covers Daphne's knee. They watch the waving kelp and the creatures that live on it, around it or nearby. Daphne makes a joke and they both giggle, leaning into each other as if whispering.

Different species of fish prefer different areas in the kelp forest. Schools of cigar-shaped, orange Senorita fish swim around the bottom of the green stems, while the silver Topsmelt live in the canopy, in small shoals. As well as food, fish also find protection amongst the kelp.

One type of fish which is often found around kelp covered rocks is the gold-coloured leafy seadragon. This solitary, independent fish appears to float between the kelp fronds with its olive-hued 'leaves' for camouflage. These 'leaves' are plant-like appendages, which hover around the seadragon. Laura would like to identify with this graceful creature. As she lifts her head, she spies a tiny nereid riding on the back of the leafy seadragon

leafy seadragon
wouldn't be the same
without the sea

it's the sea water
that holds the green leaves up
keeps them floating
and filling the space

that gives this dragon
its golden magic
between the kelp fronds

All these animals make their home here, while others visit often. Visitors include Pacific white-sided dolphins, and even black and white killer whales. These orcas bring forth a shining display by splashing up white water, as they dive to rise again.

Laura is now roused by the splashing of the orcas. She encourages Daphne, then they swim to the water's surface. Laura touches the shell in her pocket as they rise.

Most of the time, sea otters live in kelp forests, so one is here. When it is asleep or at rest on the surface, it wraps kelp fronds around its body, so it doesn't drift away. The two women are delighted with this idea, trying it out for themselves. This way they can let go, rest and watch what is happening.

The sea otter lies there on its back, with wet fur, and its paws lifted, showing its whiskers. It has a thick pelt to keep it warm, to make up for having no blubber. From the floor of the kelp forest, it eats sea urchins, bright pink or purple balls of spikes, as well as abalone, from their iridescent, mother-of-pearl shells. It balances a flat pebble on its chest, using it as an anvil to crack open its prey.

Spiny sea urchins attack the kelp holdfasts, so it's beneficial that the sea otters keep their numbers down. However, colourful asteroid starfish and small, one metre horn sharks also eat them.

The two women leave the sea otter, untie their kelp fronds and dive down again to the sea floor. They love the experience of water rushing past. It makes their hair stream out behind them. On the way down, they pass blue sharks in addition to a solitary Garibaldi. It is bright orange with a down-turned, frowning mouth. It's as if Laura is looking at a mirror that represents most of her life, if not just now. She laughs a little.

As well as sea urchins in various colours, the women see patterned sun stars and fan worms, which live in tubes made of sand. They also discover sponges of all shapes and sizes, and sea squirts, which have water-filled sacs for bodies, never moving from one place. Both women are glad they have ventured forth, as they enjoy travelling. All these animals filter their food from the water.

There are also spiny lobsters, which eat dead animals. They are known to migrate across the sea floor in long lines of more than 50 lobsters. Predators are deterred by loud screeches, which remind Laura of Daphne.

Laura muses that kelp forests contain many habitat niches. They provide food for animals, including fish, protection and places to hide among the waving fronds. Caught off-guard, Laura begins to feel muddiness throughout her being. As well as this, a brown cloud seems to hover near her.

Seagrass Beds

The two women swim on, with Laura encouraging Daphne, although Laura is still fighting off the brown cloud that has been wafting around her. As the water becomes deeper and calmer, they near the seagrass beds and Laura begins to feel better. Then they enter another kind of green forest.

In this place, there is giant seagrass about four metres long, growing on the muddy bottom. As it is a plant, it only grows at depths where light penetrates, forming dense cover. It is anchored with roots as well as having horizontal stems under the mud, stabilising these sediments, and vertical stems above them. However, the vertical stems are pushed to the side by currents.

The role of the seagrass in stabilising the sediments means that it prevents erosion. It also buffers coastlines against storms.

As Laura touches her shell, she becomes aware of the gentle dynamics of this place. Seagrass provides food as well as shelter for many animals. Most animals just visit this seagrass meadow, but some use it for one of their life stages. Many young fish live here.

Seahorses and pipefish are unusual, in that they live their whole lives in the seagrass. The prehensile tails of the golden seahorses hold onto the seagrass blades for support. They suggest to Laura the way Daphne clings to things that she loves, things and people.

It's not so much that Daphne looks to people for support, though she does on occasion, but she can also be generous in the extreme if she chooses. She will give away her most treasured object to someone who would benefit from it, or she will give spiritual healing to comfort someone who needs it.

The pipefish mimics the seagrass to camouflage itself, swaying with the blades in the current. Both pipefish and seahorses suck tiny animals into their tube-shaped mouths.

Daphne wants to know how these fish differ from the leafy seadragon, found amongst the kelp. Laura tells her that they are similar, but they don't have the olive-coloured "leaves" that the seadragon has.

Laura goes on to describe how some fish, such as herrings, lay their eggs on the green seagrass blades. As well as fish, the seagrass is a nursery for mussels as well as bay scallops. Their larvae eat the seagrass, but the adults are filter feeders. At low tide, the seagrass is grazed by coastal ducks such as Widgeon and Brent geese.

Daphne starts to look around her. She gathers some empty shells as well as some short strands of seagrass. She twists the seagrass, then pierces the shells with a broken piece of rock she brought with her from the kelp forests. Then she threads the seagrass through the prettiest shells to make a necklace for Laura. Laura is enchanted. Then, with spiral shells, Daphne makes some earrings for herself.

Laura is fascinated by the wide range of creatures that lives here, from large to small. Many species of algae, micro algae and bacteria, in addition to invertebrates, grow on the actual living seagrass leaves. Other invertebrates grow between blades or in the sediments. Some of these invertebrates are green like the seagrass, others are striped, green on green, or black and white, or black on brown.

Larger animals, such as crustaceans and snails, eat these creatures as well as the algae. In so-doing, they keep the seagrass clean. This promotes growth of the seagrass, but some creatures eat the seagrass itself. In turn, all these animals are eaten by even larger creatures. In the end, the seagrass supports a huge biodiversity.

Daphne is not paying attention. She is splashing around near the surface, enjoying the sensation of the warm water on her body. Daphne thinks the sea was made just for her.

Laura keeps stroking her shell, discovering that the only purely herbivorous sea turtles, the hefty adult green turtles, eat mainly seagrass. The only herbivorous marine mammals are the sea cows known as dugongs or 'sea pigs', who also eat seagrass. Sea lions rest in seagrass beds, with dolphins swimming over the top, together with Nereides on their backs.

It is said that dolphins were born of Amphitritte, the Queen of the Nereides. They were called the sea-nurslings of the Nereides, who looked after them while they were young.

Nereides not only ride dolphins, seahorses and seadragons. They also swim on their own. They are as quick as the blink of an eye or the glint of sunshine.

Laura is excited about all the glorious creatures found here. Some of her exhilaration spills over into affection for Daphne, so she touches Daphne's shoulder, but Daphne pushes her away. As Laura can't understand this, she is hurt. She becomes pensive. Then, she offers to give Daphne a lift on her back. However, Daphne makes a cutting remark. This slows Laura down for a while. The retort wasn't necessary; moreover, she didn't like it at all. Then, she tries to give advice to Daphne, with the best intentions, but this only makes Daphne defensive.

Laura returns to the world around her, the world that enthuses her. Her shell tells her that there are 72 different species of seagrass in the world, coming in many different shapes and sizes. Their ecological roles are reflected in their common names, which include eelgrass, turtle grass, shoal grass, tape grass as well as spoon grass.

Then Daphne demands to look at the seahorses, but Laura is afraid she will disturb the timid creatures. However, Daphne lays down the law. She enforces what she's saying with rigid hand movements. She can be quite authoritarian at times.

She has a scheme to sneak up on some seahorses and to quickly grab one, so she can hold it. She wants to feel the texture of its skin. Touching surfaces is an interest of hers, but she is often rather rough when it comes to living things.

Daphne is bossing Laura about. Laura's edges are being knocked off. Laura's own desires are not being recognised. Doesn't she matter? She doesn't know how to put these feelings into words. She runs her fingers through her hair. She can't ask for what she wants, yet she probably wouldn't obtain it.

Like A Seagrass Blade

swaying
like a seagrass blade
in the current

she feels
like a wimp
without a spine

and yet the seagrass
is anchored in the sand
but she is not

she is floating free
and unsettled
without firm foundation

a punch bag
a dishcloth
for people
to walk on

Laura loves Daphne and thinks that Daphne loves her. However, Daphne is not acting in a very tender way and Laura wonders why. Daphne can be affectionate when she chooses, so why is she not choosing?

Laura is hurt as well as perplexed, while not knowing how to react. She becomes anxious. Her head is tight; it is full of dark sand. Her chest and her arms are tense. Then she begins to be aware of a severe headache.

Daphne grabs at a seahorse, but she can't catch it. It's a surprise for the women that it is nimble enough to dodge her hand. Laura is thankful, because she has visions of the animal wilting in Daphne's fat, little hand.

Laura's headache becomes worse now, as it feels as though her head will split open, like an earthquake tear. She starts to vomit so she leans over. Yellow and green lumpy fluid convulses out of her mouth and floats around in the nearby water.

All at once, Daphne starts to whine. She is tired as well as weak. She cannot centre herself or discern things around her so these problems make her disoriented. She starts to panic, the whine turning into a scream. Laura cannot do anything to help. She has her own problems, continuing to throw up.

After some minutes, the vomiting stops so Laura wants to rest. However, Daphne has stopped screaming and started crying. Laura cannot bear the crying. She puts her arms around Daphne to comfort her, rubbing her back in a circular motion at the same time. The weeping stops, but Daphne has a red, screwed up face. What's more, it takes a long time for her to settle down and come back to normal.

The two women spend several days in the seagrass. Once Laura's headache goes, she sees again the brown cloud of depression she first saw in the kelp beds. Now it descends over her and through her. She doesn't feel like doing anything. Nothing interests her. Even things that she normally loves, like swimming, as well as watching the effects of light on the seagrass, don't enthuse her at all. This brown cloud with inertia is familiar. Something must change.

After some time, Laura's mood lifts. The more they swim, the more improved she is. Moving around helps. They decide to travel on to explore the coral reef nearby.

Coral Reef

Although Laura has been unwell, she likes over-arm swimming, as it's forceful in pushing ahead. Daphne prefers breaststroke, but sometimes she uses sidestroke. This parallels the way she keeps her emotions in close to herself, for security. Her body is curled up as she tries to protect herself. Then, as soon as something deteriorates, she can't hold everything in any more, and it all explodes.

Soon, they come to the coral barrier reef, so-called because it forms a barrier to movement to and from the coast. There are reefs like this all over the world, yet thanks to Laura's shell, they all seem to be here at once.

The two women swim close together to discover exquisite submarine gardens filled with a variety of intense hues as well as an abundance of life. Every now and then, a school of brightly-coloured fish, or a solitary fish, suddenly darts past, then there's another one in a divergent direction.

Laura wonders whether the coral, being more solid than the kelp or the seagrass, will provide more of an anchor for them, a firm focus for their attention. She would like to escape from emotions for a while, as she feels she is starting to dissolve into the seawater. However, she discovers that the reef can be prickly and uninviting, at times.

There are two main forms of coral: hard and soft. Hard corals create rock-like skeletons, which make up the structure of the reef. On the other hand, soft corals don't have these hard skeletons. They look like vivid plants or graceful trees.

Coral Reef

it's the fish
that dart
and then again
that seem
to give life
to the coral reef

to add
a higher level
to the choreography

a new colour
to the picture

Laura continues to rub her shell, discovering that all different shapes are represented among the hard corals, including a tongue and a brain coral, and an antler coral. Soft corals include black corals, which are feathery, with others having the appearance of mushrooms or fungi. Leathers are 'wavy' as well as 'wiggly' in three dimensions, and Xenia appear to be stalks with heads. Star polyps live up to their name, in addition to Zoanthid, which look like either flat discs or grids. These waters are low in nutrients, therefore, quite clear so that the mixture of brilliant colours can easily be observed.

Laura and Daphne swim over and through the coral, then a yellow tang passes by. The fish looks pure and clean. Then they see another yellow fish, this time with horizontal blue stripes, a coral like a tree as well as another coral like a fern. Here, the reef is orange and black with touches of red. Sponges project themselves outwards with open mouths.

The two women see masses of lacy orange tendrils which they realise is a cup coral consuming a juvenile octopus. This octopus is white, speckled with blue, as well as flaccid.

Just as Laura starts to enjoy Daphne's company, Daphne says something that stings her heart. Perhaps this is a defensive strategy, perhaps Daphne doesn't want to be too close. This reminds Laura of the tentacles of the coral that contain stinging cells. After stinging their prey, they eat it.

Most corals form colonies, but cup corals are solitary. This is like Laura, who is used to spending most of her time on her own. She holds herself aloof from Daphne, only doling out small amounts of company now and then, treasuring her independence. Daphne clings to her, holds her arm, always wanting more of her, but when she has too much closeness, she reacts with stings.

Coral reefs are almost self-sustaining as habitats. While seaweeds are rare, there are no plants. Coral reefs are completely made up of animals in a vast array of different forms. These include the giant clam, which is more than a metre across.

In one place, several kinds of tiny organisms form thin mats on the reef surface. These mats are eaten by gastropod molluscs, such as sea hares, which can release coloured ink, as well as by sea slugs.

These slugs are more becoming than their name implies. They are often colourful; some have aqua and black stripes with a touch of orange, but they are slow moving, just like Laura. She holds her stress deep inside, giving herself a backache. The other prey of the sea slug consists of sea anemones as well as corals, from which the sea slugs take their stinging cells. These cells then protect the sea slugs, so they are bypassed by predators.

Laura's shell says that other coral eaters comprise the bright-coloured Emperor Angelfish and the pastel-coloured Parrotfish. After eating coral, the Parrotfish expel fine white sand, which is washed up by the waves to be deposited to form beaches. At night, the Parrotfish surround themselves with a protective shield of mucous. This blocks their scent as well as disguising their shape, so that they remain safe.

Both women sometimes do similar things with their emotions, to protect themselves, which makes communication as well as intimacy difficult between them. Laura doesn't want to be stung any more, but if she doesn't listen, she won't know what Daphne is saying. She might miss out on something she needs to know.

Daphne has been defensive, either tightening her barriers or lashing out, ever since she was raped. This is understandable, but hard to live with. If the women had more insight into their own behaviour, they might attempt to change.

There are fish on the reef, of every colour. The Surgeon Fish is powder blue and dazzling yellow; Squirrelfish come in vivid reds and oranges. Many fish have quite distinctive patterns. Cleaner fish clean parasites from larger fish, which tolerate them well.

The Clown Anemone Fish, which has bright colours with white bars or patches, inhabits the swaying, pink tentacles of sea anemones, which protect it. Sea anemones feed on free-swimming animals, but the Clown Fish secretes mucous as a cover, preventing the anemone's stinging cells from firing. This is the kind of protection that Laura needs: something that stops Daphne's poison at its source.

Other kinds of fish have intriguing names, which Laura is fond of, such as butterflyfish, damselfish, seahorses, snapper, grunts, pufferfish and scorpionfish. Seahorses are often ridden by laughing Nereides, who delight in all the various hues and shapes around them.

The worst predators, such as moray eels, which have a very good sense of smell, come out at night. Eels live in crevices in the reef during the day.

Hunting in packs, black tip reef sharks are up to two metres long, says the shell. They are agile as well as being able to ram their snouts into minute gaps. The women can't believe it. The sharks frighten the small fish out of the coral, then eat them.

Another inhabitant of warm reef waters is the sea turtle. Laura and Daphne find it wondrous that such a big ponderous creature can swim with so much grace.

Being flexible, octopus can also squeeze into tiny gaps. They are intelligent, changing their colour for camouflage.

Like the octopus, and like the water, which surrounds them, the consciousness of the two women can enter small openings in the environment. Their awareness, together with their empathy, seem to infiltrate and permeate animals, as well as plants, where there are plants, along with inanimate things.

This means that the women are sensitive to the most diminutive changes around them. Their consciousness seems to flow like water between them as well as to all other things. This signifies that, when the women are completely in touch, they are aware of soft feelings; moreover, they are gentle and flexible in their responses to events, just like the graceful undulations of swimming fish.

However, sometimes this sensitivity and awareness can bring them pain, prickly feelings or despair. This happens often when they misinterpret each other, or when events from the past linger in their memories. However, the deep muddiness of depression doesn't bother Laura while she is on the reef. The diversity of colours as well as forms here delight her.

in the sea
there are stripy things
moving quickly things
waving around things
brightly coloured things
dull looking things
staying still things
popping out and snapping shut things
hanging on and sucking things

things with whiskers
things with frowns
flat things
long things

green things
curly things
simple things and
very complex things
smooth things and
rough things
soft things and
hard things

and

undulation

On occasion, however, Laura does feel pricked by the reef. This is because something is bothering her deeply, which she doesn't want to face.

When this happens, she finds comfort from the variety of hues as well as patterns, which abound on the reef. Banded shrimps are bright reddish orange and purple. Sponges are each a colony of animals, coming in a great number of forms. Sea fans look like seaweed, or a river delta with many tributaries. They are, in fact, one form of soft coral.

Laura and Daphne are sad to leave the coral reef. They would rather stay here, but they have committed themselves to a journey, so they move on to the nearby shallow seas.

Shallow Seas

Laura is inspired by the rich, abundant life in the shallow seas, at all different levels of the food chain. Her heart beats fast, her breathing is rapid, and her eyes open wide as she looks around her. As well as the residents, there are seasonal visitors who come in to this place when there is plenty of food.

The residents include porpoises as well as dolphins, who breathe air, therefore needing to be near the surface most of the time. However, they can also dive to the bottom of the ocean, often taking Nereides with them. Close knit pods of relatives live as well as hunt together. They use echolocation to find prey as well as for navigation, so they can explore all the nooks and crannies of their environment. In addition, they use sound to communicate with each other.

Their prey comprises open water fish as well as squid. They herd the fish into a ball near the surface of the water, taking it in turns to eat. Sea birds, together with sharks, also come for the feast until nearly all the fish are gone. The women find it a spectacle.

Porpoises are smaller than dolphins, lacking their prominent beak. Living as well as hunting in smaller groups, they are less acrobatic. The two kinds of creatures are often found together, but Nereides prefer to ride on the backs of dolphins. As the Nereides lean forward, their long red hair streams out behind them.

Suddenly, Daphne starts to be rude to Laura. In fact, Laura feels that Daphne is being hostile. She is assaulting her with aggressive words. Laura can't understand why. What is going on? Daphne says she is winding her up, moreover she intends to go ahead with teasing her.

Laura remains calm but says she isn't in the mood to be teased. She knows she probably wouldn't ever be in the mood to be teased like this. She is under attack.

Daphne says this is how she was brought up. Laura says she doesn't have to stay that way.

Anger rises in Laura's body. She is so hot, so vigorous, seeking the truth, wanting to express it. What has she done to deserve this?

Then, Laura attempts to suppress the rage, so she can proceed with discovering more wildlife. However, her subconscious, which is still angry, interrupts her. The subconscious knows that Daphne wants Laura to be quick, so it slows Laura down. Laura is not conscious of this, but she can't move fast. Is this what is called being passive-aggressive? Her resentment is demonstrated by lack of action.

Laura's wrath surfaces again. She starts to think about leaving the journey or travelling alone. She could enjoy the sea creatures well on her own. She doesn't like being stung or harassed or kicked around. She hates being taken advantage of or carrying the burden of someone else's moods. She has enough problems with her own emotions.

On the other hand, perhaps she should just give up and go home. After all, they have seen a great deal up to this point. They have explored the coast, consisting of the surf, the sandy beach, the pebbly beach, the rocks, the sand dunes, the estuary, the cliffs as well as the mangroves.

In addition, they have investigated the coastal waters, including kelp forests, seagrass beds, the coral reef and now, shallow seas. In the process, they have encountered all manner of intriguing kinds of wildlife.

Nothing else could be as thrilling as what they have already seen. What could be better than the subtlety of an abalone shell, or the scampering of a crab, or the subliminal wistfulness of the estuary, or the colourful hues of the coral, or the grace of the leafy seadragon or the rich diversity of the seagrass beds? What could be better?

The purpose of the journey was supposed to be personal growth – growth which would improve the relationship. Maybe she would just have to give up on that. It would be a pity, but there you are. It might just have to go.

She pauses for a minute. She takes a deep breath. After all, she did pride herself on her belief in commitment. Commitment would mean finishing the journey with Daphne. How would Daphne cope without her? Daphne wouldn't be able to finish the journey without her. She would be distracted by a side issue. Would Daphne be able to find her way home?

Then, Laura starts to think about what lies ahead: the freedom of the open waters – that would be refreshing, the wind to blow the cobwebs away, clever camouflage, large sea creatures, fast sea creatures as well as frozen landscapes. She would love the whiteness, the birds, not to mention the polar bears of the polar regions.

Perhaps she could continue. Bit by bit, she starts to see that her problems are not as overwhelming as she thought.

You just need a broader perspective, she thinks.

Her mental excursion has given her the time out that she needed. She turns back to Daphne but doesn't say a word about what she has been thinking. Her attention goes back to the wildlife.

Laura's shell passes on information about killer whales as well as barracuda, who are high-speed predators, who live in shallow seas. They make Laura and Daphne nervous. The women's pulses quicken while they draw in their breath. The killer whales are also known as orcas being, in fact, the largest dolphin species. However, Nereides won't ride on them. They are the most widely distributed mammal in the world.

The resident dolphins live in large pods. They hunt using their voices and have diminutive home ranges. The transients, or visitors, live in small groups. They hunt in silence while they travel over a wide area. The residents specialise with their choice of prey, usually eating certain types of fish. Other dolphins sometimes travel and hunt with the residents.

Barracuda are snakelike in appearance, with sharp-edged, fang-like teeth, much like piranha. No wonder the women are anxious.

Sea lions are seals with ear flaps, but they can lift their bodies off the ground, while seals can only shuffle along. Both creatures have long whiskers which help them find prey in the dark or in turbid conditions. These whiskers make them look attractive to Laura and Daphne.

The rays include the electric ray as well as the torpedo, which generate electric charges to stun small fish. Daphne would like to experience the electric charges, but Laura won't let her.

In the waters above the sea bed are found shoaling fish, all of which filter the sea for plankton, while concentrating in huge clouds that block out the light. Sea birds like gannets dive like guided missiles to catch fish. In addition, dolphins and sharks are attracted to the shoals, and sometimes even a whale. Whales that eat fish wander the ocean to find seasonal, coastal abundances. Minke whales are much smaller, eating coastal fish all year.

The great white shark has mottled or patterned colouring on its back. Laura's shell tells the women that it is the largest predatory fish, up to six metres long, weighing up to two tonnes. It eats other sharks, dolphins and turtles, and seals. Its custom is to attack from below, with jaws wide, to kill or disable with a single bite. Then it retreats to wait for the prey to weaken from blood loss.

Sometimes, Laura feels that Daphne is like the great white shark. One cutting remark from Daphne makes Laura feel destroyed, as if she has been disabled with a single bite.

The killer whale occurs in both coastal and offshore waters. It is also known as the orca or grampus. Near the coast, it feeds on fish as well as other small prey, but in the open ocean, it harasses to kill much larger whales including humpbacks. Daphne harasses Laura, even though Laura is taller and thinks that she is more sophisticated.

The women see a killer whale leaping in a vertical line, out of the water. There is a great deal of white water shining in the sun, reaching to half its height. The black and white killer whale is sleek.

There is also a clear, black silhouette of a bat ray against bright sunlight. It has a soft, round snout, two triangles for wings, and an extremely long, thin tail. It feeds on the seabed, but it moves with grace through open water.

The electric ray is fawn with dapples of charcoal. Its attractive appearance belies its sting. It has a disc-shaped body with a long tail. It lies in wait on the ocean floor for small fish to approach. When the prey is close enough, the electric ray envelops it with speed, with its body as well as firing off an electric charge to stun or kill it. Then it feeds.

Laura equates Daphne's defensive remarks with this sting. The comments usually stun Laura then hurt her so that she clenches her gut muscles. Daphne is trying to protect herself, it seems, but her speech is dangerous. Why does she need to protect herself, anyway?

Conger eels rest by day in sneaky crevices on the seabed, emerging at night to feed. These ugly creatures are some of the longest eels, up to three metres in length and as thick as a human thigh. They can savage humans.

Shallow Seas

there is no stillness here
not even within

there are stings and bites
and fish that block
out the light

then the excitation
of dolphins at play

Laura loves it when a school of little fish swims near the surface in a dark circle, with bright light from the sun coming through the centre. Light plays with water in myriad ways.

Open Ocean
Clear Water

When the women leave the safety of the coastal waters, they discover the freedom of the open ocean. They take deep breaths so they can let go of their worries. Vast areas of water surround them.

As Laura strokes the shell, she realises that the open ocean covers over half the Earth. It is the second largest of the world's habitats, after the deep sea.

However, it is low in nutrients. The water is clear but not nutritious. Therefore, it contains little life. It is the marine equivalent of desert.

Like a desert, the shell says, it contains oases, or spots where surface water is carried out from the coasts or where currents well up. These oases contain more nutrients, together with more life. This appeals to Laura, but the oases shift, carrying the life they feed with them. Like a shifty person, they are not dependable.

Uncertainty

no thing to stand on
no direction to go in

shaking in the body
water down the legs

Laura is disconcerted by the idea of oases. She prefers it when things can be defined and even tied down, as many creatures are on the coral reef. She likes swimming in the ocean, which is changeable, after all, but as a rule, she knows what to expect. Even change which is predictable is easier to handle than uncertainty. Her shoulders sag at the thought of it.

Her depression, which is getting worse, takes the form of immobility. With it comes a fear that she will stop all together. This is a dreadful prospect.

However, she keeps rubbing the shell, as if for security. It has become familiar and that comforts her. The shell is just the right size and shape for her hand, and despite the repeated massaging, it hasn't lost its shape or its surface texture. This lack of change brings her contentment.

The shell tells her that because of the shifting nature of food, predators here who feed on plankton often swim large distances to find prey. In these well-lit waters, there is nowhere to hide, so fish employ more imaginative strategies. These consist of travelling in shoals for protection, where only outside fish are picked off. The tactics also include having streamlined bodies, so they can leave at speed. Cryptic coloration makes all creatures, including fish, harder to find.

Daphne is also unsettled here, as there is nowhere to hide. Her red hair is like that of the Nereides, but it makes her obvious. She would like more patterned coloration, but as this is absent, she moves sideways when confronted. Even her thoughts are lateral, always approaching the matter in hand from a novel direction.

This demonstrates intelligence, but is difficult for Laura to comprehend, because she is logical and linear in her thinking. She often finds she can't understand Daphne at all.

One case of inexplicable behaviour is when Daphne makes a sudden announcement. She accuses Laura of dominating her. Laura feels as though she has been hit in the chest. Everything she does is with Daphne in mind. She cares for Daphne, so she tries to look after her. She would never hurt her.

Laura does things for Daphne only because Daphne cannot do them for herself. Either, Daphne is asleep, or medicated, or in emotional pain, or cannot speak because of her asthma. Laura communicates on Daphne's behalf, in these cases, but won't any more.

A full revision of Laura's behaviour is necessary. She must inspect herself in detail, so that she can change. Nevertheless, the sense of injustice stays with her.

The fish in the clear water may be fast but the predators are faster. They also have fine eyesight for close-up views. In addition, their other senses help them cope with distance in the vastness of the ocean. These predators can be a great size: they include the world's largest animals.

Laura feels rather as if predators are 'out to get her'. She feels crushed by Daphne's criticism; besides, when she thinks about it, she is at a loss, in real terms, as to what to do about it.

Wind

Waves grow as they cross the open ocean. Now, a huge wave breaks in a cascade of white water then falls into still, smooth, blue waters. Then again, Laura sees light catching the inside curve of a wave.

Her shell tells her that waves move through surface water, not with it. The water particles within a wave move in a rough circle as it passes.

Body Surfing

the inside curl
of the wave
is blue

as the white shimmer
hangs forever
about to fall

the human body
is raised
and carried

by the pressure
of a huge balloon
underneath

this buoyancy
nurtures the body
like a wave of bliss

Laura caresses the shell in her pocket. Surface currents which flow, laden with nutrients from coastal regions, are known as 'rivers in the sea'. They are maintained by prevailing winds, sometimes travelling for thousands of kilometres. Nereides ride in them for a while, then change.

As Laura strokes the shell, she remembers the Gulf Stream, which journeys from the Gulf of Mexico across the North Atlantic to Britain and the Norwegian Sea. Its volume is 500 times that of the Amazon. As well as nutrients, it carries warmth, which affects the entire climate of Northern Europe. It supports within it many animals.

Often, Laura is carried along in a stream of life, without any say. She is buffeted by circumstances just as waves are made choppy by the wind. The whiteness of the caps on the surface of the water is caused by bubbles and droplets reflecting sunlight. Laura would like to have more control over her own direction. She longs for things to change.

Nutrients in the surface currents feed phytoplankton, which come in all varieties of shapes. Laura can only see them with the shell, because they are so tiny. Some of them are orange, green or blue, together with several pink circles. Others are rectangular, and a good deal of them are long and thin. All kinds of complicated forms are represented.

Also, many marine invertebrates, including worms, molluscs and crustaceans, have planktonic larvae. These join the stream of life transported by currents to colonise new places.

Jellyfish also travel with tides and currents. As well, they move with rhythm, by pulsating their bells, to maintain a vertical position in the water column. Most species of jellyfish feed on fish as well as other free-swimming animals, which they catch in their trailing tentacles. These tentacles contain stinging cells which immobilise then kill their prey.

This is just how Laura feels when Daphne attacks her. Sideways, underneath the conversation, Daphne's remarks can sting Laura like a sharp needle. Laura bends over in pain. This is even more so because the remarks are undeserved.

In their turn, Laura recalls from her biology studies, jellyfish are prey for leatherback turtles, one of the world's largest living reptiles. Mature individual turtles are greater than 2.7 metres in length, weighing almost a tonne. Because of this weight, they need to follow ocean currents. However, they dive for food.

Laura is privileged to see one of these turtles passing by, as they are rare. The head, body, shell and flippers are all covered with blue spots. The top of the shell is a corrugated ridge.

Laura's shell rubbing tells her that many of the world's ocean surface currents join up to form loose circles called gyres. These currents are driven by prevailing winds as well as being influenced by the rotation of the earth. In the centre of the gyres, parts of the ocean achieve stillness. In one case, Sargassum seaweed floats freely on top of the water, in great rafts, forming a forest habitat, which is a hiding place for fish.

Laura likes the idea of ocean stillness, but the seaweed reminds her how tangled living can be. What is more important, her relationship with Daphne or her relationship with her mother? Laura wonders whether these connections even affect each other. How can she make her way through the kelp of life to the still point at the centre?

Wind

it's not the wind
that we love
but the lack of it

the still point
at the centre
resonates
with stillness
in our hearts

magnifies it
and brings it
to our attention

The shell helps Laura to see that at the edge of the Gulf Stream, eddies form as enormous swirls of water. Seen from above, spirals of light emerge from the expanse of more solid light.

Not only does Daphne love spirals, but so does Laura. She sees them as a symbol for spiritual growth. They move in repetitive circles that keep changing a little, getting smaller and smaller as they approach the still point in the centre. An illuminated one like this resonates with the light in her heart.

Then Daphne farts loud and long. Bubbles spread away from her. Laura is mortified. She tries to think that it wasn't deliberate. Then she hears Daphne laughing. She sounds free and happy. Daphne's head is thrown back while her chin is lifted. A grin lights up her face. Laura's own heart contracts. She would like to leave the situation.

Shoals

Time passes. Laura doesn't forget what happened, but she puts aside her negative thoughts.

The two women play with the idea of invisibility. They watch what the fish do, swimming with them.

If fish are discovered, they bunch together, seeming to act as one. Each fish follows and mimics the one in front, but very fast. Each fish has its own instinctive response to danger.

Many shoal fish are coloured or patterned, so they are harder to pick out. The women notice the silver mackerel whose upper sides have iridescent blue and green stripes. This helps the fish blend in with the rippling surface of the sea. It is harder for seabirds to spot them from the air.

In some cases, the silvery sides of the fish reflect light, making their bodies seem to blur together. So, patterns and reflection are two strategies. A third is transparency.

Laura is mindful of the many marine invertebrates that are nearly invisible. They are transparent, therefore less likely to be seen. One of these is the jellyfish, which can thereby escape predators as well as catch prey. They live near the top of the water column.

One species of jellyfish is called "by-the-wind sailor". It has an air-filled float, along with a sail of transparent tissue above its body, by which it catches the wind. Beauteous Nereides love to play with it. They sing in delight as they play.

Laura keeps stroking her shell, almost with absent-mindedness, discovering that larvae, the early form of some animals, are small, slow and without defences, compared with adults of the same species. Therefore, invisibility is the best strategy for survival, being achieved by transparency. This applies to the larval blenny fish, the larval squid as well as many more larvae.

It can also be achieved by adult creatures like the pram bug and the hydromedusa. The semi-transparent pram bug females attack and eat salps, hollowing out their bodies. When they have laid their eggs in the shell, they propel it through the water like a pram. The hydromedusae are a kind of jellyfish.

Tiny sea gooseberries with their 'bike helmets' and their long tails, are also transparent, says the shell. Even large swarms are imperceptible from any distance.

So are swarms of salps almost invisible. These tiny creatures have long strings, or they have spiral shapes or wheel shapes.

The reason Laura would like to be invisible is that she would be absorbed into the spiritual. Nothing would exist except inner light. It would be like bringing, with reverence, the celestial inner world out, to replace the everyday world.

to be invisible
is to be clear
and hard
as a diamond

to be invisible
is to be strong
like a river
in the centre

to be invisible
is to be shining
from within

Some fish leave the water, as Laura would like to do sometimes, when she is desperately longing for change. When she doesn't know how to handle a situation, she wants to leave.

Needlefish leap through the air for some distance. Flying fish spread their fins, gliding. They beat their tails with vigour, from side to side, travelling up to 150 m.

As Laura's shell tells her, the largest fish to leave the water is the short fin Mako shark. This shark can weigh up to 1,000 kilograms as well as being 4.5 metres long. It is the fastest species of shark because it can reach 74 kilometres an hour. The speed aids in leaping so that it reaches about nine metres above the water. Its brilliant, metallic blue back glints in the sunlight. Laura wishes for its power as well as its height.

She would love to fly as well. She believes flying would open a window of light in her being. The exhilaration would be inspiring.

At that moment, Daphne starts to cry. She is hiding behind her red hair, sobbing for no apparent reason. When Laura asks her what is wrong, Daphne shoots out a cutting remark that stings Laura. Daphne replies that Laura knows, she must know. When Laura shakes her head, Daphne repeats herself.

Laura is at her wits' end. She puts the palms of her hands up to the sides of her head. She feels her frustration might lead her into depression. She doesn't know what to do.

After more discussion along the same lines as before, in the end, Laura discovers that Daphne's asthma is bad. Did Daphne expect her to hear her wheezing or did Daphne expect her to read her mind. It seems that the latter is true.

This also explains Daphne's defensive behaviour. She does, in fact, expect Laura to know what is happening for her without being told. As Laura doesn't know, she doesn't express any caring or do anything to resolve the issue. Daphne interprets this as negative behaviour.

Great Size

Many huge creatures live in the open ocean. The women are overwhelmed by them, although the problems of understanding each other seem just as large sometimes. They wonder whether they will ever resolve them.

Some Nereides bring the women a certain kind of seaweed, which relieves Daphne's asthma. After resting and partaking of a distillation from the crushed seaweed, Daphne feels much better.

Laura rubs her shell. The biggest animal that ever lived on earth is the blue whale, which is rare. While its heart is the size of a small family car, an adult human could swim down its biggest blood vessels.

Its first exhalation, or blow, is filled with water droplets. Because the blow can rise nine metres above the waves it can be seen from some distance. The women marvel at this display. They wish they could 'let off steam' like this.

The blue whale is solitary. Laura, too, has been solitary for many years before she met Daphne. Because of this, Laura doesn't understand about resolving issues before they build up to a large size. She doesn't catch on about being assertive as well as standing up for herself. Since she has seldom done it, she doesn't know how to go about it.

Laura massages her shell. As well as the blue whale, the fin whale is also very large but travels in groups. It is also more acrobatic. Laura and Daphne try to imitate the acrobatics. Exercise like this should help them relax, besides, it looks like fun. Sometimes, the adult whales can be seen breaching, leaping their bodies almost entirely out of the water.

The humpback whale has the longest flippers of any animal. They are more than 4.5 metres long and are used to communicate. The whales make a huge noise by flapping their flippers against the water surface. In addition, they sometimes lie on their backs holding their flippers in the air.

The shell lets them listen to whale songs, which are long and complex, with identifiable patterns lasting more than half an hour. The whales use snores, groans, chirps and whistles as well as other sounds, repeated sometimes for hours. These tunes, which can be heard 160 kilometres away, are used to impress females. There are regional dialects, along with subtle changes from year to year. They delight the women, who then try to choose their favourites.

The three-note song of the male blue whale is the loudest noise made by any animal on earth. It can drown out a jet engine, travelling for hundreds of miles. To the women, it is the equivalent of a Buddhist chant, so that they feel like bowing down in reverence. They kneel and bow.

Then, Laura strokes her shell. The oarfish is the sea serpent of myth. Because it has a long sinuous body like a snake up to eight metres long, it has been mistaken for a sea serpent.

Laura is curious, touching the shell again. She becomes aware of supposed sightings of sea serpents. One has been reported to lift itself up like 'a column from the water'. It could crush boats and kill humans, along with blowing water in a curved spout.

Poseidonius said his sea serpent had jaws 'large enough to admit a man on horseback' as well as having flaked, horny scales. Several reports describe the sea serpent as 20 metres in length. It could travel up to 105 kilometres per hour.

Claus Magnus said that the sea serpent resides in rifts as well as caves. It eats calves, lambs and pigs and, when it is in the sea, sea nettles, crabs and so forth. It has long hair, sharp black scales together with flaming red eyes.

One myth says that the Sun and Moon were hatched from two crimson sea serpent eggs hidden in a willow tree. One of the symbolic meanings of the sea serpent is transformation. Laura resonates with this information. Strange as it may seem, it makes her feel at home.

She keeps tuning in to the shell with her fingers. Kundalini comes to mind. Kundalini is a coiled serpent of spiritual energy seated at the base of the spine. When it is stimulated, it travels up the spine to the head, causing transformation. Laura keeps this information safe for future reference.

At Angkor, in Cambodia, there is a statue of a meditating Buddha, protected by a multi-headed naga, or serpent. Laura is attracted by the stillness and silence that the Buddha conveys.

Another myth tells that the Buddha was meditating under a tree. The serpent king, Mucalinda, came from his abode among the roots of the tree, to protect the Buddha from a forthcoming tempest.

The venom of the snake is associated with providing expanded consciousness, supplying the Elixir of Life which gives eternal life, and bringing immortality through divine intoxication. Laura almost stops breathing.

Serpents are also associated with entheogens, says the shell. These are plants or other substances which generate the divine within, thus leading to spiritual experiences, which, in turn, lead to spiritual development. Because of this association, the serpent is believed to be one of the wisest animals, with closeness to the divine.

Laura and Daphne continue to swim among the huge creatures that wander through the open water. Laura rubs her shell. The whale shark is the biggest fish in the sea with a huge mouth at the front of its head. It is docile, being harmless to humans.

The manta ray is the largest of the world's rays. It has two enormous lobes on the sides of its mouth which help direct water and prey to the opening. Often gathering in big groups, the manta rays use grace to flap their muscular 'wings', which are up to 4.8 metres wide. The women enjoy this strange ballet.

Laura is thinking about Daphne. She is considering how Daphne carefully observes body language, so that Laura can't elude her at all. On one such occasion, Laura was trying to help Daphne with her dressing. She was feeling sorry for Daphne, looking down on her a little for not being stronger. She was trying to keep these feelings from Daphne, but Daphne knew at once. Daphne reprimanded Laura with acrimony.

Laura takes her attention back to the creatures around her, touching the shell. The sunfish called 'mola mola' basks at the surface of the sea. Its enormous body is round as well as flat, with almost no tail. It can be up to 3.6 metres long, weighing more than a tonne. The women join it in the sun.

The most terrifying fish is the short-fin Mako, seen earlier by the women. It has long, backward-pointing teeth that jut from its mouth like fangs. Suddenly, Daphne sees the fish when she least expects it. She screams. Laura anticipates that Daphne will recover from her fright, but that doesn't happen. Daphne continues shrieking and screeching.

Laura is stunned. She can't think what to do. She doesn't know why Daphne is screaming so much. Perhaps there is a hidden reason that makes her vulnerable to terror, an underlying anxiety. Daphne doesn't explain that this huge fish looks like the hallucinations that she has at night.

Panic is rising within Laura. What is she supposed to do? Daphne doesn't want to be dominated by her, yet she needs some help. Laura doesn't want to do anything in case it is misinterpreted, as usual, making matters worse. She feels her pulse rate rise, while heat and energy fill her body. She is breathing too fast. Tension grips her. Her panic makes her want to leave, to escape as soon as possible.

Speed

Two dolphins leap in big curves out of the water. They leave white water as well as spray behind them. They inspire Laura with their exhilaration so that she notices two laughing Nereides, one on each dolphin.

Laura has suppressed her panic as much as she can. She took some deep breaths, letting some time pass. Although she remains shaky, still feeling the urgent effects of adrenalin in her system, the Dolphins and the Nereides take the edge off her unpleasant emotions.

Now, she is looking at animals that move with speed. They stimulate her adrenalin even more, although she doesn't move much. According to her shell, the fastest creature in the ocean is the cosmopolitan sailfish. As streamlined as a dart, it can move at 109 kilometres per hour. It uses broad muscular sweeps of its tail, with tail fins shaped like a V. These give it great acceleration.

It takes Laura's breath away. She can't keep up, as her feet seem to be weighed down. This is a psychological effect due to the many unresolved issues both with Daphne and with her own mother. Laura is repressing not only her anger, but also her internal conflicts. It is too much, so she needs to change.

The sailfish is three metres long. While in clear surface waters, it hunts squid, tuna, jacks and needlefish, all of which are also very fast. As it enters a shoal of fish, it sweeps its long bill through the water with the intention to stun or maim its prey. Momentum takes it out the other side of the shoal, but it returns for the prey it has hit. Daphne stuns or maims Laura's emotions whether she intends to or not. However, the effects of her words are probably deliberate.

Its dorsal fin is like a sail that can be raised and lowered like a flag. In this way, it frightens its prey. Another terrorising tactic is that it changes colour in pulses as it attacks. Similar predators are the swordfish, which is migratory, as well as the marlin, which has a spear-like snout or bill.

Trying to catch her breath, Laura is struck by a thought.

It seems I have made a mistake in choosing Daphne.

This thought averts the depression which was about to fall on her. This is because she is being honest with herself.

With her mind on these other things, Laura fondles her shell. Dolphinfish are prey for these other bigger fish. They have a brilliant metallic blue-green body. Juveniles travel and hunt in shoals very close to the surface. They lie in wait beneath rafts of seaweed for flying fish.

Among the most streamlined of marine mammals, says the shell, are spinner dolphins. They twist on their axis in the air several times when they leap out of the water. Laura wonders whether the Nereides would be able to hold on to them while they do this.

All sharks have a superlative sense of smell. Their nostrils are used solely for smelling, not for breathing. They home in on blood. With a torpedo-shaped body, one of the fastest sharks is the blue shark.

However, the short-fin Mako is even faster. With great speed and power, it can outrun the blue shark. The prey of the Mako is swordfish as well as yellowfin tuna.

Known for its enormously long tail fin, the thresher shark works in pairs or groups to herd prey. They circle schools of fish, then stun them with swipes of their tails. Laura feels stunned often, usually because of something Daphne has said, something that doesn't fit properly in Laura's view of the world.

As Laura continues to stroke her shell, she finds that dolphins also hunt in groups. The common dolphin moves in schools of up to two thousand, often swimming with yellowfin tuna. The dolphin hunts squid, along with smaller fish. It is a powerful, fast swimmer, excelling with acrobatics. On numerous occasions, it leaps from the water, somersaulting in the air for enjoyment. These activities are often accompanied by Nereides. Wishing for the day when she used to be energetic, Laura sighs. The world seems to be moving too fast for her, right now.

The striped dolphin is even faster, as well as more acrobatic. It can lap six metres from the surface, leap upside-down, doing backward somersaults in the air. Dolphins are famous for being playful, which is why Nereides love them, but they sometimes jump to communicate. The noise from the dolphin's body hitting the surface registers a certain distance.

With the bottlenose dolphin, all the dolphins mentioned so far are typical dolphins. They have teardrop shaped bodies, prominent dorsal fins, rounded foreheads as well as obvious beaks.

The killer whale is sometimes classed as a dolphin. It even hunts other cetaceans. One instance of this is when killer whales in a pod will work together to kill a baleen whale calf. To start with, they try to separate the offspring from its mother. Then, they take turns riding on the calf's back to prevent it reaching the surface to breathe.

Laura despairs at this cruelty, while scratching her head. She believes in God but, if God created the natural world, a great number of vicious practices were included. What kind of God could this be?

Speed

breathing too fast
beings that leave
their shadows behind

accelerating darts
changing colour
like disco lights

brilliance
of metallic colours
streaking
around corners

the cry of the child
without its mother
the creature
without restraint

Polar Seas
Cold Comfort

Antarctica

in the shapes and textures of white
and the pristine savage silence
we find the inner structure of pure mind
and the awe-full coherence of primordial crystal

The women discover the cold, polar landscape, so now they slow down a great deal. The cold temperatures give them quite a shock as they are used to warm waters. However, due to the general magical quality of their journey, they can make the transition successfully. Part of them transcends such petty differences.

They rise to the surface of the water, then Laura touches her shell. The polar seas are productive waters. In summer, it is light all day as well as all night. This makes microscopic algae and other phytoplankton grow, feeding large numbers of crustaceans and fish. In turn, these are food for breeding colonies of marine mammals and sea birds.

Laura too, is much happier when she is productive, writing poetry. She gathers a great deal of inspiration in this environment.

In winter, there is little sunlight, even none for months. In the dark, phytoplankton shut down production, dying back. Only a minimal amount remains, most larger creatures leaving for warmer places, only to return with the sun. With them come the Nereides.

However, the polar waters are bitterly cold even in summer and are often encrusted with ice. Nevertheless, Laura finds purity and order in the cold. The focus of her attention comes right back home to herself.

Laura's shell can reach to the north or south with equal ease. There is a polar ice cap at each pole, pack ice and icebergs. On the ice, polar creatures such as the leopard seal can be seen resting or raising their young.

Iceberg

in several orders of magnitude
greater than our minds can hold
the noble monument
slides through the water
and the sky
blessing the air

on its shaggy tufted sides are
whiskery crenulations
but
its lustre is implicit triumph

It may have been stressful travelling to this destination, but both women find great encouragement from the icebergs, now they are here. They feel quite out of breath with excitement.

The bergs are not seen anywhere else but here. Besides each one is different. While most of them are as big as buildings, each one is at a different stage of melting. Young icebergs are still craggy with a great deal of detail in their surfaces. As they start to melt, they become smooth as well as rounded. Some have stalactites of ice hanging down in the mouths of their ice caves, to look like fairy tales.

Blue ice fills the interiors of the icebergs. Some are so rounded that they appear to have tunnels leading inward to blue regions. This kind of image lends itself to metaphors, as if the blue ice represents the subconscious mind. Both women are enchanted by this location.

Laura and Daphne enjoy sharing these experiences. Participating together enhances the encounters with the icebergs even more. Each one points out her new discoveries to the other one. They laugh at the way the sea creatures, as well as the marine environment, always parallel what's happening for them. Currently, they are both spell-bound, so much so that the spell binds them together.

Above It All

seen from above
cold chunky Antarctic clouds are like
the hot rugged rocks of Arnhem Land

scarred and lined
and surrounded by a sheer drop

Laura and Daphne watch huge numbers of avians flock to the polar areas. These winged creatures migrate to arrive in spring to breed. Laura wonders what nesting habitats the birds are looking for and rubs her shell.

In the Arctic, birds nest on islands as well as northern coastlines. On escarpments, the thick-billed murres can be found, as well as black guillemots, which contrast with the white landscape. Tufted puffins, which have red-orange feet and bills, make burrows in the cliff topsoil. Their tufts are like hair swept back behind their ears. Cute auks, in their black and white attire, live among the rocks and boulders on steep slopes.

All these birds drift on the waves in huge rafts diving from the surf to catch prey underwater. Although they all have short, stubby wings, they are graceful underwater. Because of the purity here, knots of tension dissolve, so the women are also aware that they are graceful. Their movements are fluid. Black guillemots, with their bright, white patches as well as their long beaks, are the deepest divers, diving to the depth of 182 metres.

Some Arctic birds steal the catches of other birds. Arctic skuas look like elegant ladies but they harry small species in the air, forcing them to drop or disgorge their prey. Their solitary nests are placed on dry tundra or rocky uplands. They defend their eggs and young with aggression, by dive-bombing predators. Laura recognises that this aggression is how she would guard Daphne if the need arose.

Ducks include eiders, which provide downy feathers, king eiders and oldsquaws. They only come ashore to breed, but they love to dive, both in the open ocean as well as onto the seabed close to shore. King eiders forage on the seabed, up to twenty-five metres deep. Oldsquaws are now called long-tailed ducks, which is an appropriate name.

Laura strokes her shell again, learning that gulls inhabit most coasts around the world. The larger ones include glaucous gulls and Iceland gulls, both of which are opportunistic feeders, even taking the eggs and chicks of other birds. Ivory gulls are daintier and have perfected whiteness. Their wings are angelic wings when they are spread open.

the melting sea ice
makes magic with mosaic
of crystal pieces
mirroring the radiance and fragility
of elfin enlightenment

Nereides are delicate but strong, so in summer, here in the polar seas, they dance to keep warm. They keep up with the shadows of the birds, timing their dances to synchronise with the flights.

Kittiwakes are unusual among gulls for their black legs, although there is a red-legged species. Their cry sounds like their name.

Terns are dissimilar to gulls. They are much more graceful fliers, combining gliding with flying. They catch their prey by diving from the air at small fish just below the surface.

The longest migration of any animal – up to ninety thousand kilometres – is undertaken by the black-capped Arctic tern, which travels to Antarctica to feed. The women's journey is short by comparison. This tern spends the greatest proportion of its life in the sunlight, more than any other creature, moving with a combination of flying and gliding. Laura also loves sunlight, but finds the transition states of dawn and dusk enchanting.

When Laura hears the Nereides giggling in the background, she realises that Daphne's mirth is just what she needs. Daphne's wit stimulates her to laugh, too, as well as to be more cheerful. Otherwise, she would be far too serious.

Laura strokes her shell, discovering that, when not breeding, albatrosses spend their lives out over open water. These huge birds glide on the updrafts that form above the crests of waves. Laura thinks this would be wonderful, to surrender to nature, letting it carry you along.

The birds roam vast distances to eat surface fish as well as squid. The wandering albatross is the larger species compared to the royal albatross. Both species fly right around the Southern Ocean, riding on prevailing winds. With a wing span of 2.5 m, they are effortless in flight, their grace seeming ethereal. However, on land, they look fat, squat and clumsy. This is how Laura feels when she is out of sorts, but not now.

Thoughts seem to come to Laura at odd moments. Now, she realises that Daphne is not the only person to expect people to mind-read. She has also counted on Daphne reading her mind, becoming angry when she received an answer she didn't want. Therefore, she has no right to criticise Daphne for this sort of thing.

She continues to massage her shell. A huge bird, the giant petrel has a two-metre wing span, and a massive hooked bill for tearing open flesh. Known as the 'vulture of the sea', it eats carrion and chicks.

The cape petrel is smaller and daintier, the size of a pigeon, with a diminutive, neat bill. However, if approached, it regurgitates a jet of foul-smelling oil from its stomach. This jet can fire several feet. Laura is reminded of how Daphne used to be, with her stinging remarks along with her bad moods, but she seems to have calmed down now.

The storm petrel is the size of a sparrow. It lives and feeds over the open ocean and is often seen winging its way in the most extreme gales. Laura would like to do this, ride Daphne's emotional storms without getting involved or hurt. Laura envies flying birds, that must be somewhat detached from the ups and downs of life because they have a broader perspective – a novel viewpoint. The storm petrel breeds in Antarctica, nesting in many other places, because it is the most common wild bird.

Sometimes, in this pure world, the women feel that they can, like the birds, rise above their troubles. Differences between them, Laura's mother's influence, Daphne's history and so on, do not seem so bad now. After a good sleep, things seem better as they do here. The women are aware of being adults rather than children. They can cope, so they stand straight. They manage to enjoy the wildlife around them.

The sheathbill reproduces in Antarctica. It doesn't have webbed feet, so it spends most of its time on the ice. It devours carrion and faeces. The women try to ignore this disgusting behaviour while wondering whether it forebodes ill.

Out in the Cold

Laura strokes her shell while the women look forward to finding out about penguins and seals. They begin by learning that many polar birds and mammals venture into the ocean to find food, but mainly live on the ice. Among these are penguins, which are only located in the Southern Hemisphere. While all species of penguins are flightless, only four species nest on Antarctica itself: the Adélie, Emperor, Chinstrap and Gentoo.

Penguins are well adapted for swimming. They are as graceful in the sea as other birds are in the sky. The women hold hands while they watch them. As well as their smooth and tear-drop shaped bodies, which give them a streamlined effect, penguins' wings act like stiff paddles. What's more, emperor penguins steer with their tails. Their feathers are small, all growing in one direction, towards their feet. Their black and white, curved colouration acts as camouflage to protect against marine predators, because the birds' own shape is not clear against the ice.

Emperor penguins walk or toboggan on the ice sheets. The women try tobogganing as well, lying on their fronts, and laugh out loud like little children when they fall sideways.

They lift each other up to try again. In the distance, they can see Nereides dancing.

With king penguins, emperor penguins mainly hunt squid by deep diving. Emperor penguins plunge up to 304 metres deep. The two species have long beaks which help them grip the squid, which is soft and slippery. Sometimes, Laura recognises that circumstances are like the squid, when she cannot grasp what is going on. Daphne usually has some insight, though.

Laura's shell continues to inform them as they observe the sea creatures. Adélie penguins, who only live on the Antarctic coast, feed mainly on krill. These small crustaceans are white and yellow with red delineation. The penguins detect them near the water surface, so they don't have to deep dive.

Emperor penguins are the hardiest creatures on earth. This is because the males endure icy months of darkness, screaming gales up to 200 kilometres an hour, and temperatures as low as -60 degrees Celsius. After two months, when the females return from fishing, the males have lost half their body weight.

Polar Landscapes

gothic winds sculpt the surface
into solid waves

pressure creates frozen dissonance
and massive glaciers
are like
movements in the eternal
archetypal white cliffs stand witness

Chinstrap penguins look a bit comical, from certain points of view, as they suit their name. With Gentoo penguins, they are related to Adelie penguins. Gentoo penguins woo their partners with carefully chosen 'love token' pebbles.

Penguins spend a large amount of time on icebergs as well as on slabs of ice because their predators are in the sea. These aggressors include leopard seals, which have large mouths and huge teeth. They are dissimilar from most seals which hunt fish or crustaceans. They lurk in the water at the edge of ice floes, waiting for penguins to return from feeding at sea. They also follow penguin shadows on the ice, breaking through from below, or they wait on the floes, catching penguins as they emerge from the sea.

Leopard seals spend most of their time in the water but give birth on the ice. Because the women love penguins, they don't want to like leopard seals, but they can't help admiring their resourcefulness.

While Laura watches the seals, she muses on her mother's behaviour all those years ago. These thoughts come into her subconscious every now and then, usually making her depressed. However, this time she remembers something different. As well as her objection to Laura's poetry, late at night, that time, which led to Laura's depression, there was one other thing that happened. Laura's mother apologised.

To start with, she apologised for keeping Laura up late and depriving her of sleep. This was straight after Laura's suicide attempt. Laura's mother tended to blame any emotional upset on lack of sleep. She had kept Laura up for two hours while she harangued her, so she pointed this out to Laura, afterwards. This was her way of saying she was sorry, even though she didn't acknowledge the harm her words caused.

Many years later, Laura's mother apologised again. It was a hint of an apology, but Laura accepted it. She knew what was intended. She also knew how hard it was for her mother to say it.

Laura's mother had never liked change of any kind. Whether it was to do with lifestyle, language, etiquette, status or morality, she didn't like to change. She was a stiff, inflexible person.

Also, Laura's mother saw herself as the teacher as well as the policeman of her daughter's habits and morality. She couldn't be seen to be wrong. She didn't ever think she was wrong. She did her very best to be good, so how could she be wrong? She often had insight into other people's actions, but not into herself. So, how could she say sorry? She used to tell Laura to apologise to resolve an argument, but she couldn't do it herself.

So, when she tried, Laura recognised what was happening. Laura's mother said, "I made quite a few mistakes, when I was younger."

The conversation was interrupted then, so Laura never knew what her mother might have gone on to say. However, Laura understood.

Now, peace enters Laura's heart. She feels calm and contented for the first occasion in a long time. Perhaps forever. She pauses to enjoy the moment. She lets it soak in to her body, to the roots of her being. Where there was separation and rejection, now there is resolution and wholeness. She recognises that this is a healing event. There is only one thing further needed.

She turns her attention back to the wildlife. While ross seals live in heavy pack ice, feeding on squid, they are the smallest, as well as the least abundant of the Antarctic seals. They are up to two metres long, the females larger. They have big eyes and they make complex, trilling and siren-like vocalisations. They call the women to stay in this enchanting place. The women are so joyous that it is easy to love each other. They find that they are hugging more than normal, as well as holding hands. They are both stimulated by the same things, which is the best basis for a relationship. Dependence is irrelevant.

The male elephant seals are enormous, several times larger than the females. The males can be over six metres long, weighing about four tonnes. They also have trunk-like inflatable snouts. One huge male fathers all the offspring on one beach area, with rivals recognising each other's voices. They eat squid as well as fish, and dive deeper than other seals, up to 1,500 metres. The females plunge deepest. These seals can stay underwater for up to two hours.

The above seals are true seals: out of the water, they are unable to move, except by shuffling bodies. On the other hand, fur seals, other eared seals and sea lions use flippers to lift themselves off the ground so they can just about walk.

The women are so easy together, perhaps because this is such a delightful place. As well, they have left ordinary life behind, and with it, Laura's depression and Daphne's crying. They are so busy here, wondering at all the marvellous sights, that they do not have time for neuroses. The joy of the natural world is their joy, the beauty, their beauty.

In the Arctic Ocean proper, there are no fur seals. There are only true seals as well as walrus, the latter looking pale in the water, but reddish brown out of the water. Both genders of walrus have tusks. They dig up clams as well as other shellfish from the sea floor, and they also find food with the help of the many bristly whiskers which cover their top lips.

They also squirt jets of water from their mouths onto the sea bottom to expose hidden prey. Laura doesn't know if she wants to expose the hidden secrets that exist in her relationship with Daphne. Some things are better left alone.

Walruses are social. In huge numbers, they haul out onto ice floes as well as rocky beaches to rest. They enjoy being packed close, with some even on top of others. They share their body heat, but Laura and Daphne are amazed. The women prefer to be solitary, either alone or the two of them together.

There are five species of Arctic seals, the largest being the hooded seal. They can be up to three metres long, weighing over 300 kilograms. The male can inflate his bizarre hood, which covers the top of his head, to intimidate rivals. The male can also force the lining of his nasal cavity out through one nostril, blowing it up like a big, red balloon.

The pups of ringed seals are hidden in snow caves. The pregnant mothers dig through the ice from below, hollowing out chambers in the snow. Here they give birth, keeping the pups for two months until they are weaned. The burrows also keep the pups warmer. The females enter the water from the caves to hunt.

Laura knows that Daphne finds the pups adorable, but Laura herself continues to be glad that she never had children. The ringed seals gain their name from their patterning of dark spots surrounded by light grey rings.

On the other hand, harp seals, also known as saddleback seals, and ribbon seals, give birth on the ice. Ribbon seals have striking coloration: they have two wide, white strips as well as two circles against dark brown or black fur. Bearded seals gain their name from their long, white whiskers.

Laura touches her shell. When standing on their hind legs, Polar Bears can be up to 3.3 metres tall. Only found in the Arctic, they weigh more than a tonne. They are solitary hunters, eating seals, most of the time, out of the water, on the pack ice.

They are land animals, but they can swim for several hours. Their feet are webbed in part and their coats are water repellent. While they paddle with their front paws, their hind legs steer. Both women love polar bears, but wouldn't want to meet one alone, without protection.

Many fish use natural anti-freeze in polar waters, beneath the ice, where the temperature is lower than zero degrees Centigrade. Some can even excavate burrows in the ice to live in to hide from predators. Both Laura and Daphne understand this need to hide, though their need is psychological. They like to escape from the world on occasion because they find the world hard to deal with. They need a rest.

Laura's shell shows them that, in both polar regions, there are some permanent holes in the ice sheet. These are kept open by upwelling currents of water that is a little warmer, which keep the surface in continual motion.

Huge cracks in the ice, called leads, provide channels for birds as well as mammals. They stay open because of movement of water in the horizontal layers near the surface. Laura and Daphne swim down some leads. In the Arctic, leads are used by belugas (white whales) as well as narwhals (small whales).

Belugas are known as sea canaries, as their communication and echolocation are full of moos, clicks, trills, squeaks, twitters and whistles. These sounds can be heard both above as well as below the water surface. They make Daphne giggle. Belugas can change their facial expressions. When vocalising, they purse their lips, which also alters the shape of their foreheads. Male narwhals each have a single long tusk, giving rise perhaps to the legends of unicorns.

Arctic cetaceans include the killer whale, minke, and bowhead whales. The latter is the largest creature to overwinter in polar waters, living off its fat reserves. Its three metre baleen plates, for filtering krill, are the longest of any whale. The minke whale is black, grey or purple in colour. Most of the length of their back, including the dorsal fin as well as blowholes, appears at once when the whale surfaces to breathe.

In summer, the phytoplankton clouds are extremely dense, assisting every level of the food chain. The sei and grey whales arrive, and in Antarctica, penguins venture further south, as do Nereides. Sei whales prefer deep offshore waters, while grey whales were once known as 'Devilfish'. This was because they ferociously defended their calves and themselves against whalers. Laura's angry actions are like this, when she thinks Daphne is threatened. All these animals have a flurry of feeding themselves and their offspring, during the warmer months.

Under the Ice

There is a complex, unknown world underneath the permanent ice, which Laura's shell reveals to her. In the Arctic, ice algae grow on the underside of the ice sheet, like mould on a damp ceiling. These species include diatoms, euglenoids, yellow-green algae, golden algae and several more. Laura always likes golden things, so with ice algae, it is the same. She prefers the golden algae, although other kinds are edible. One species hangs down in green strings like submarine Spanish moss.

These algae make Laura think of how subconscious matters exist below the surface of the mind without many people knowing. The psyche is hidden a great deal of the time, but this is where change needs to happen.

Here, under the ice, it seems that Daphne likes the poetic style that Laura uses. Daphne smiles when she reads Laura's poems. Most of them seem to tap into the subconscious.

These mould species, and phytoplankton, growing under the ice, are eaten by zooplankton which are swallowed by copepods which are eaten by Arctic cod. The largest jelly-fish in the world, the lion's mane jellyfish, also lives here. The diameter of its bell is 2.4 m, and its tentacles, which look like raw meat, are 30 metres long. There are also several kinds of squid.

Laura strokes her shell, which shows that the world's second largest predatory shark is the Greenland shark, a sleeper shark. This family of sharks obtains its name from their apparent slow swimming and their low activity level, together with their perceived non-aggressive nature. Usually, the Greenland shark does take its time, just like Laura, but it has sudden frightening bursts of speed. It has a wide range of prey. It hunts beneath the ice as well as in open water, also scavenging on the seabed for such things as bodies of whales.

The Arctic Ocean is shallow, compared with other oceans, being less than 1,200 metres in depth. There are plenty of icebergs, including small ones called growlers. In Antarctica, there are black mountains, covered, in part, with snow.

Polar Landscapes

silver birch-like mountains are background
to seraphic unheralded monoliths

subtle finesse is august and rugged
in the cold steel of the albino landscape

Holiness

huge black peaks
pointing upwards
from the white all around

black pyramids
articulating the sacredness

of the landscape

untouched
the ice generates
pure order

a long forgotten
Himalayan
origin of thought

    This poem refers to qualities of Laura's meditation, which give her stillness. She almost stops breathing. The other thing which supports her is the way Daphne listens to what she says. Daphne will listen to a conversation about almost anything, ponder what has been said then give good advice. This means a great deal to Laura.

    Daphne expresses her liking for Laura's poems. In her eagerness, she leans forward. She finds the Antarctica poems evocative and is fascinated by the metaphor of the ice representing purity. Daphne usually prefers different figures of speech to those of Laura, but, in this case, she can understand Laura's point of view. She tells Laura that she is a poet of the sea.

    The polar seas are full of visual images. Humpback whales have lumps like giant callouses on their heads as well as on their flippers. These lumps provide anchorage points for barnacles which live there for their adult lives. On the other hand, the common seal has a cute appearance because of its whiskered face as it emerges from the water, surrounded by soft ice. The women don't want to leave this place.

Storm

However, the women do leave the polar seas, heading towards the equator. Their relationship has been going so well, that Laura bends to kiss Daphne. Their speech to each other is quiet, in their own playful language. They stroke soft cheeks, only just touching. Laura cups the back of Daphne's head in her hand. They move closer. Their mouths open as they continue kissing. They lie down. Their arms entwine as each holds the other. With tenderness, they make love. Light shines through them, while the peace is palpable as they lie in each other's arms. The warm glow is kind.

Then Daphne asks Laura for some money to pay her bills. The anger rising in Laura dirties the atmosphere. Her whole body is clenched.

What a grubby thing to say!

Laura dares not express her anger out of respect for their lovemaking. However, it eats away at her.

When Daphne repeats her request, Laura bursts out with everything she's been holding back. She is so angry. What does Daphne think she is – the client of a prostitute or something? She thought they had real love between them but now it feels so dirty. Why can't Daphne pay her own bills, anyway?

They find out later that it was a White Squall that knocked them over. Out of the blue, with no clouds in the sky, fast wind lays them flat. When it passes, they try to collect themselves together.

Then it starts to rain. Tiny drops fill the air like mist. Then there's a sudden burst of a heavy deluge so that all the sea creatures disappear. The black clouds overhead begin to resound with lightning and thunder. Wind whips up waves, higher and taller. There seems to be no difference between the sky and the sea.

The torrent turns to hail. Wind blows ice from the side so that it stings their faces, their naked legs. They are tossed to and fro. They have left the polar seas behind them. They are thrown off balance.

Laura blames Daphne for causing the storm, with all her sharp barbs. Daphne accuses Laura of dominating her as well as always attributing fault to her, instead of taking responsibility for herself. Laura hates Daphne's grossness, her laziness. All the negativity comes out. Daphne returns that Laura is also lazy, plus she has no sense of humour. Laura is a coward because she won't face reality. Laura wonders how Daphne knows these things that are supposed to be secret.

The raised voices are harsh, strident. Fingers are pointed, arms are waved against the wind, with the wind. Faces are focussed sharply in accusation. Breathing is faster, hearts are thumping, temperatures rising.

Both women are frightened, but Daphne is terrified. She feels that all the forces of nature have turned against her, so she re-interprets everything that happens to fit that scenario.

She sees visions of sea-monsters, bizarre fish with very large teeth, which she swears are real. She is shaking all over.

The women call on the nereid Queen of the Sea, Amphitrite, for help. She comes, flashing bright radiance from her eyes. She has the power to still the winds and to calm the sea, but in this case, she is interrupted by Nemertes, the wisest of all the sister Nereides.

Nemertes is known to give unerring counsel, but this time she is stern with Laura and Daphne. They must be brave because of what is coming, they must face themselves, especially Laura. It is important for her growth. Daphne needs healing from a terrible wrong so Nemertes will give her counselling. Both women must stay with the storm.

As soon as Nemertes stops speaking, billows knock the women over and under. Then a fast wave comes and joins a slow wave and becomes a rogue wave. This new swell is much bigger than the others around it. The rogue wave knocks them over again. It pushes them underneath it. The weight of the water in this huge surge creates pressure, which thrusts the women deeper into the abyss of the ocean.

The Deep
Alien world

Laura and Daphne arrive in deep water. Daphne is accompanied by the nereid, Nemertes, who now begins to give her counselling. Laura hopes that Daphne will pour out her heart about everything that has ever mattered to her.

Laura's shell still functions, even here. It tells her that the average depth of the ocean is more than 3.2 kilometres. Below 198 metres, everything is black. In the open water, life is sparse, so predators must make the most of every meeting. The long teeth of the viper fish increase its chances. Both the fish and its teeth have a translucent, pale blue quality. Should one be afraid of this fish? Because of its appearance? In this surreal world, any mistake could result in a searing wound.

The Deep Sea is an alien world with crushing pressures and absolute darkness. There are unseen terrors, such as monstrous squid, huge sharks and bizarre fish. This nightmare world is like the women's subconscious, with surreal images everywhere they look. Many species seem to have no skin. They look like muscle with internal organs. This is how Laura feels, naked and stripped bare by the storm. She can't hide any more, now. She can't conceal anything now, not her weaknesses or vulnerabilities, not her faults, not her history.

The Deep

surreal visions come to life
soundless distortions of reality
pangs in the body
cold on the skin
creeping inside and out

then no skin at all
just organs and muscles

exposure lets the heart out
racing
forcing
pushing

silent as death
twilight zone changes
and flickers
nothing is the same

cold as death
steel in the deep
all should be frozen
but texture moves

    Because of her nakedness, the pressure of the water, and the darkness, Laura is forced to face herself. She is in disarray, as well as having no energy to put on a role. She can only be herself.

Laura discovers that when she thought she was being serene, she was, in fact, being lazy. She was afraid of hard work because it made her body feel unusual, stressful.

She found that she couldn't cope with pain. She just wanted it to stop, to go away. That meant she was a coward.

Laura liked being private, even secretive. She liked finding hidden meanings in life, but this quality signified that she was deceptive. She sometimes told lies.

Again, what she thought of as firmness, commitment and perseverance implied that she was stubborn. She was psychologically stuck, she wouldn't change. She needed to be flexible so that she could grow.

Daphne was right, as well. Laura always blamed others where she should have taken responsibility for herself. Laura was full of criticism for Daphne, but, until now, she didn't see her own faults. This was because she was trying to come to terms with imperfection in the world, and therefore sounding critical, but it had a detrimental effect on other people. She became a negative, lonely person.

Open Water

Lanternfish are prevalent in deep water. They, like many other inhabitants of this realm, produce their own light. They have rows of light organs on their body and head. This makes Laura think of the spirituality of inner light.

Jesus said 'I am the Light of the world', and sometimes this Light shows itself. Nevertheless, in this place, each species has its own individual pattern of light organs, suggesting that they use them to recognise others of the same kind.

The flashlight fish has a pocket beneath each eye which contains glowing bacteria. Hatchet fish have rows of organs along their undersides, which emit light. Their bodies are vertically flattened so that they are difficult to see from above or below.

Laura brushes the hair back from her face. As depth increases, sunlight disappears with speed. This is because water acts like a filter, absorbing the different wavelengths as well as colours that make up white light, one by one. The first to go is red, then orange and yellow. Greens and blues penetrate further. Below 198 metres, there is no light at all.

In the transition zone, which is blue, many creatures are red so are therefore invisible. Red pigment absorbs blue light well, for photosynthesis. Red seaweeds, together with red algae, survive much deeper than green ones. Below 198 metres, even these disappear. The women make their way, deeper into the ocean and deeper inside themselves.

The Sea is a dream, but it has seemingly lucid moments. Daphne is well into her counselling now and, in addition, the Nereides nurture her. Anything is possible in this dream, the Sea. The Nereides give Daphne sea treats to eat and drink, including sushi as well as various types of marine algae. There seems to be a magical boundary around all the food, so that sea water doesn't dilute the flavours or ruin the textures. The sushi is vegetarian, composed of vinegared rice and vegetables, wrapped in kelp and served with soy sauce, wasabi and pickled ginger. Daphne relishes the sushi with the salty soy sauce, but her special favourite is the warm, spicy and sour taste of pickled ginger.

The algae include some kinds of ice algae as well as red, green and brown algae. Some of the red algae are Carageen moss, grape stone and nori. Some of the green algae are green caviar and sea lettuce. Some of the brown algae are Kombu, Wakame, Sargassum and hijiki.

All the algae are ingredients in delicious vegetarian dishes, which have the additional flavour of the sea. She is also offered some sea snails, scallops, and mussels, as well as oysters and squid, but she declines. She has come to know these animals as friends. To drink, Daphne has Kombu cha or seaweed tea, with its strong, familiar fragrance. Magically, it pours from the pot to the cup in one stream, ignoring the watery environment.

The Nereides also massage her with several kinds of massage. Some of these massage types work more on the physical body, others work more on the emotions. The entire rub-down routine takes days. All things are possible in this dream, which is the Sea.

The Nereides begin with Swedish massage therapy, which uses lotion or oil, along with following Western knowledge of physiology. Daphne relishes the feel of the oil, which must be good for her skin. Oil and sea water don't mix and through a magical exercise of will-power on behalf of the Nereides, the oil adheres to Daphne's skin, instead of rising to the water surface.

The Nereides follow this with aromatherapy massage which utilises fragrances from all parts of the ocean. They put Daphne into a dream state. Hot stone massage warms Daphne's tense body as well as improving her circulation, while the stones stay hot because of the same kind of magical focus of the will. Deep tissue massage relaxes her sore muscles.

Shiatsu uses the same pressure points as acupuncture, without the needles, and follows meridians, or lines of energy through the body. It doesn't use oil. It is based on the principle that psychology and physiology are connected, so it may release emotion. The hard pressure is not to Daphne's liking, but afterwards she is aware of energy moving in lines of light through her body. This is delightful.

Thai massage combines acupressure, Indian Ayur Vedic principles and assisted yoga postures. Ayur Veda uses oil in the selection of food such that when Daphne is feeling anxious, it is recommended that she eats oily food like cashews and other nuts. Warm sesame oil is used for the massage, testing the magical powers and mind control of the Nereides. Keeping the oil warm at this great depth of the ocean is difficult. The Nereides themselves are in their element.

The stretching of the yoga enlivens Daphne's consciousness. The Nereides finish with reflexology on pressure points on Daphne's feet, without oil. This makes her tingle all over, especially in her head.

Through this process, Daphne releases some deeply held emotions, so they no longer affect her. Among other things, the counselling helps her to continue to let go of these feelings and to replace them with positivity.

The Nereides also brush her red hair, streaming out in the ocean water, together with warming her body with their body heat. They continue for many hours and days until Daphne's self-esteem returns. It seems that she has recovered in full, from the bad treatment in her past. Only a faint scar remains, at the base of her emotions. She can remember what happened, but she is no longer hurt by the memory.

Light decreases as the women go deeper into the ocean. On the other hand, pressure increases with depth. It is one atmosphere at the water surface. Just ten metres below the water surface, the pressure is doubled. Another atmosphere is added with every ten metres beneath. Near the bottom of the lowest ocean trenches, the pressure is a thousand atmospheres. This is equal to 10,000 tonnes per square metre.

Laura feels unbearable pressure to cleanse herself. She presses the palms of her hands onto the sides of her head in frustration. She looks like the figure in the painting of *The Scream*, by Edvard Munch. She must cast off all negative thoughts, unravel all knots of tension.

Deep sea animals naturally maintain internal pressures equal to the pressure outside. Some fish have gas-filled bladders that they use to control their height in the water column.

Laura tries to replace her negativity with positive thoughts. She can manage to see some good things about her mother. These include her mother's wonderful ways with gardening, her kindness, her hard work. She always rose in the mornings, never slept in.

Laura is compassionate, so she remembers how she put some time into looking after her mother when her mother was ill. This gave Laura a chance to know her better as well as to improve her understanding of her. She learnt that she and her mother were similar in some ways or had been in the past. She had many of her mother's mannerisms. She discovered where she had gained certain traits, such as tilting her head to the side.

She also experienced that they were completely different in other ways. She realised that her mother was childlike, in some ways, even at her advanced age. She still couldn't cope with poetry. However, her mother was good and desperately tried to be virtuous, and to see herself as moral and upright.

Laura stands still, addressing her thoughts to her mother.

Dear Mum, I love you to pieces. I remember what you were like and how much I loved you, a long time ago when I was tiny. I hadn't yet begun to see that you had faults. I hadn't started to separate as an individual. You were milky white and shining. I loved you with my whole heart and my entire being, with everything I had.

The first thing that happened was that I perceived your limitations. You didn't always say the right thing. I was hurt by that perception, then angry. I was disillusioned about you as well as disappointed.

However, you still loved me. As I tried to change into an adult, or rather from a child, you and I had many struggles. Even though I disagreed with you, and perhaps you were wrong, you were motivated by affection.

I think you were wrong about poetry. You were misguided to be angry with me that night. You were perverse to keep me up late, and to blast me to smithereens, to attack the essence of my soul as well as to take away my reason to live.

You expressed hatred of me while I was so close to you that I couldn't bear that hate. You rejected me. Your word was absolute, so because of that, I rejected myself.

It seemed you were trying to destroy me, to kill me, so I went along with that will. I also wanted to escape from all the pain and from all the twisted confusion that overwhelmed me.

No wonder I thought you wanted to kill me, when you had come running out, calling for the carving knife. It was frightening. Death hung in the air, over everything.

I must have defused the situation. I ran outside to warn my friend and that gave you the chance to collect your thoughts. It gave you the opportunity to realise the enormity of your proposed actions.

Then you had to justify yourself to me. You had to explain why you were so angry. You did this by talking to me for two hours – I didn't say a word.

Laura's attention comes back to her environment. She finds it hard to think about that night, so she sits down, caressing her shell with an absent mind. It tells her that below the transition zone, there is a vast habitat. It covers more than half the Earth's surface with a depth of about 1.6 kilometres. It is like the air between the land and the clouds, except that it is pitch black as well as full of living creatures.

Most zooplankton migrate at night to be near the surface, so they can feed on phytoplankton. Otherwise, these as well as other marine creatures eat what is called "marine snow". This is made up of tiny pieces of organic matter that drift down from higher levels. Marine snow nourishes zooplankton, which feed prawns and small fish.

Some fish make the nightly journey up to higher levels with the zooplankton. One of these is the hatchet fish, which is shaped like an axe. The colour and intensity of the light that the fish produces are equal to that of the light coming from above. However, this fish light is not visible from below.

The shell continues. Other fish use light to attract prey. One of these is the anglerfish, which has a luminescent lure. It can eat victims almost as big as itself. Some fish live on the seabed. One of these is the monkfish, which looks like a small rock covered in vegetation. Laura is a monk, too. She is stripped down to the basics, pure and simple. She is here for just one purpose, to resolve her issues.

Laura continues to address her mother.

Mum, now I can see your motivation. You were doing the best thing you knew how in the circumstances. You thought in all honesty you were trying to protect me, to guard me from immorality. You were trying to save me from some terrible wrong-doing.

You had an inappropriate feeling that you had a duty to be responsible for your offspring's morality. This was out of proportion, not to mention no longer your obligation, when your daughter was an adult.

You were always very emotional but this time, it was extreme. As you were on a roll with passion and certain thoughts, you didn't know when to stop.

That was part of your character. What happened usually was you kept going until things became ludicrous, over the top, then you lost perspective.

Laura takes her attention back to her shell as well as the creatures around her. Gulper eels have ribbon-like bodies about 60 cm long, but they could swallow something the size of a basketball. Some of them have bioluminescent lures on their tails.

Flashlight fish have so-called eyelid shutters over luminescent pouches. These pockets help them to see prey as well as to attract it. The pouches are shuttered when the fish are in danger.

Most bioluminescence is blue, but the loosejaw fish generates and sees red light. It can see its prey without being seen. It also has long, sharp, backward-pointing teeth so that the prey can't escape. The vision of this fish is horrific, so Laura hates to look at it. However, because of her special shell, she can see everything. She can't avoid seeing anything. She must face reality, in all its aspects.

The most spectacular teeth are those of the viperfish. As well as a snake-like body, the teeth are long fangs. Laura shudders with horror. The stomach is elastic, covered by a dark film which shades the bioluminescence of its meals.

Bristlemouths are relatively small, but are the most abundant fish in the sea. Their luminescence is like that of the hatchet fish.

Laura is drawn back to address her mother again. If she can reconcile with her mother, she will become a different person, a stronger person who can deal with Daphne more easily. The depths of the maternal ocean seem to be a good place to work through her issues with her own mother.

Yes, Mum, you used to lose perspective. But you couldn't see that. And you didn't foresee the consequences of your actions, that is, my depression as well as attempted suicide. You wanted to destroy my actions, and I think on one level, you wanted to destroy me. But perhaps not on another level. You were angry, but you were still my mother. But you were ignorant because you didn't know what you were doing.

It is hard for me to forgive you. But I do, because of the love I used to feel for you, as well as on the foundation of the love and compassion I felt for you in your last years, as I related to you as an adult, not to mention my awareness of your faults and hang ups and circumstances that restricted you. These circumstances included your lack of experience with this situation, as I was your only child, your upbringing, your own dominating mother, society and the church. It was vital to you that everybody else think well of you along with your family. I also forgive you on the grounds of your ignorance of the effect of your words and actions, as well as because of your apology and what it must have cost you.

I FORGIVE YOU. I forgive you. I forgive you because it is the loving thing to do, because I can let go, because I can't hold a grudge not to mention because it was all a long time ago, because it is over.

The eyeflash squid migrates upwards at night. The colour of its bioluminescence changes with the temperature of the water. It is blue in colder, deeper water but it turns green in warmer, shallower water.

Laura loves the colours. She is glad to have resolved things with her mother, even though her mother is no longer here. Laura is more loving as a result, as well as lighter. She has lost a weight she has been carrying around with her for many years.

Some squid flash their organs of light to startle attackers. One of these is a squid which has large, yellow light organs on the ends of its two longest arms. Laura is certainly startled when she sees it, even though she is not an attacker. Nevertheless, because she feels stripped bare, as well as, because she is in the painful process of facing herself, let alone because she has just let go of a heavy weight, she is in a vulnerable state and oversensitive to everything around her.

She can see that both the giant squid and the colossal squid are far larger than any other invertebrates. Her shell tells her they are more than 18 metres long.

The shell goes on to say that the giant squid is an active predator, finding its prey by smell in the dark. However, it uses its large, well-developed eyes in the twilight (transition) zone.

The colossal squid lives in deep water in polar and sub-polar seas. Its two longest arms end in clubs covered with swivelling hooks. Laura wants to scream but no sound will come out. The squid's arms also have large, circular suckers to grab prey and pull it to its mouth. This mouth is a huge beak like that of a parrot. The principal predator of both these huge squids is the sperm whale.

Sperm whales are the greatest deep-sea divers. They need oxygen, but they hunt more than 1.6 kilometres below the surface, for up to two hours. They can do this because they use oxygen from their muscles as well as their lungs with high oxygen efficiency. Laura is somewhat jealous of them.

They find their prey by echolocation, by focussing their loud clicks into a sonic beam. Laura is learning to focus her attention. Sperm whales are the biggest active predators in the world, measuring 18 metres in length and weigh 50 tonnes.

There are also the seldom seen pygmy whale and the dwarf sperm whale. The former is, in fact, a dolphin. The latter is the most diminutive true whale, being smaller than the bottle-nose dolphin. There are also 20 species of beaked whale. They are great divers, eating squid. The females have no teeth, but the males have two or four large ones, which grow up from their lower jaw. Laura likes to plunge with the females, but the appearance of the males, with their big teeth, puts her off diving with them.

Laura fondles her shell as it continues to inform her. A few comb jellies live at a depth of 3,300 metres. Some of them are pleated and folded as well as semi-translucent. Laura notes this with delight. She returns the shell to its new home, in a tangle in her long hair.

The tube-eye or thread-tail fish looks naked. It is just sinews and bones with a large, opaque eye. It hangs in the water column waiting for little prey, such as free-swimming crustaceans, to move past. When it spots some prey glowing, or silhouetted against the distant surface, it expands the huge pouch below its lower jaw to suck the prey into its mouth.

Laura doesn't like feeling naked and exposed like the tube-eye fish. Without any clothes to have pockets, she needs to keep her shell in her hair, but she still feels vulnerable. However, the next step is to feel clear and translucent, like the comb-jellies. She looks forward to this.

Some shrimp and squid fill the water with bioluminescent material which dazzles predators. In this way, they have a chance to escape. However, all the surrounding water is filled with light. Something like this happens soon.

The Deep Seabed

The women arrive on the deep seabed. Daphne has been healed from her wounds, moreover, because of the counselling, she now has a new attitude to other people. She is not so self-centred. She can see other people's points of view, together with showing that she cares about their well-being. This includes rubbing Laura's back when Laura is tired or vulnerable.

Laura has changed as well. Because she has faced herself as well as dealt with her feelings towards her mother, she is now humble, besides better able to give love. She welcomes Daphne back into her sphere, with a sincere hug.

Laura discovers that her special shell works equally well on the deep seabed, which is more than 3.2 kilometres down. The seabed is made up of vast plains, plummeting trenches and steep-sided mountains, which haven't been altered in millions of years. This makes Laura consider ancient truths, which stand the test of time. Here there is total darkness; complete silence and cold.

Of the animals here, some are the same as those found elsewhere. Others are bizarre or living fossils. One example of the latter is the coelacanth, which hasn't changed in 400 million years. This time span overwhelms Laura. The coelacanth is a lobe-finned fish, and it's a living member of the group that gave rise to the first vertebrates to walk on land.

Laura thinks that this place must be near the origin of life. When she thinks, she is aware of a thought before it becomes verbal. Does this mean she is close to the source of thought?

Hagfish are scavengers which have no jaws. They tie their flexible eel-like bodies in knots to rip chunks from dead animals on the sea floor. They are reddish pink and grey, snaking their way through the skeletons of carcasses to pick their bones clean.

Laura remembers the symbolism of snakes. There is supposed to be a female serpent of subtle substance coiled at the base of the human spine. This serpent can be wakened, bringing about change.

Sharks are generally more primitive than bony fish, but ancient sharks are even more so. They have not changed in 420 million years. This time span puts everything into a different perspective. Laura sees that the matters she is worrying about are not worth it.

The ancient sharks have no large, front dorsal fin. They are slow swimmers, as Laura is listless. They stay close to the seabed, as well as having a good sense of smell.

Another shark in this realm is the bizarre-looking goblin shark, which is more than three metres long. It has a snout like a fleshy shelf together with a jaw that juts out. It is a creature of nightmare.

Laura notices that she is not as frightened as she used to be. She is no longer as sensitive, but she retains her greater sense of empathy. She is now more confident to face potential danger, knowing somehow that she can handle it.

Facing her prior conflict with her mother and resolving it, has removed a great deal of built-up animosity. This has cleared a path for different thoughts and new strategies for dealing with life. It has made way for novel means of experiencing herself, as well as the world.

Other sharks live near the seabed but feed in open water. They include lantern sharks, which have luminescent mucous covering their bodies. Laura wonders what this would feel like. Would it be good to shine? The green lantern shark is the smallest of all sharks. It hunts in packs for deep-sea-squid which is larger than itself. In groups, the green lantern sharks harass it, gradually wearing it down.

The cookie cutter shark takes bites out of large animals, including the sperm whale. The cookie cutter shark can detect electric pulses, using this ability to catch its prey. Laura wonders whether she will ever feel electricity.

The megamouth shark is a filter feeder of plankton, jellyfish and squid. Its enormous gape shows the inside of its mouth, covered with tiny luminescent organs, which may be used to attract prey. Its large mouth reminds Laura not to speak too much in this silent place.

Deep sea rays use their electro-receptive sense to find prey under the seabed sand and mud. Laura also loves to explore things that are hidden, most often hidden meanings. Their prey consists of bony flatfish such as left-eyed megrim as well as right-eyed halibut.

Invertebrates are more common on the seabed than fish. Echinoderms have hard plates of calcite in their skin for protection, which Laura wishes she could have. Instead she will have to continue to develop strength of character. The adult echinoderms can't swim. They include starfish, feather stars, sea lilies, sea urchins, sea cucumbers as well as brittle stars.

There are over 1800 species of starfish, Laura realises as she strokes her shell. They prey on bivalve molluscs such as scallops. The suction pads on their tube feet pull the shells apart. Laura thinks that a great many good things, like this, are a slow process. The starfish ejects its stomach into the gap to digest the flesh inside. This process may take hours or days.

Feather stars have many feather-like arms, which have bristles. Laura no longer feels she has bristles. Hers have dissolved when she faced her innermost feelings. She has released her stress. The feather stars intercept the organic 'marine snow', which falls to the seabed. As sea stars are slow, feather stars also move in a deliberate manner, with the tiny legs under their arms. On abyssal plains, which cover more than 50% of the earth's surface, feather stars almost fill the seabed.

Sea lilies are attached to one place by a flexible stalk. On top, there is a sideways "parachute" making them look like a flower, even though they are an animal. Nereides love to play with them.

Sea urchins have protective, mobile spines. Laura now has all the protection she needs, coming from within. With their many tube feet, the spines help the sea urchins move at their leisure. They taste the water, following the trail of particles until they find their food.

Sea cucumbers also move at leisure along the seabed, sucking up sediment. They expel the inorganic matter. If harassed, they fire threads of sticky material from their anus, which disable or distract predators. Some sea cucumbers have a transparent outer body, giving them an alien appearance. Laura feels transparent throughout her entire body.

Brittle stars have much more flexible arms than starfish. They move faster by comparison.

Crustaceans, such as lobsters, crabs and prawns, also live on the seabed in large numbers. Some grow to large sizes which amaze Laura. The heaviest is the North Atlantic lobster, which ranges from 20 kilograms to the size of the average five-year-old child.

The Japanese spider crab, which lives for a hundred years, has a leg span of 3.6 metres. Laura is no longer daunted by these huge crawling creatures.

Squid live in open water and shoal. On the other hand, octopuses hug the sea floor and are solitary. One species flaps huge 'ears'. Most octopuses are small, but one species is 3.6 metres long, weighing more than 61 kilograms.

In mid-ocean ridges, molten rock surges up and heats water to a great deal more than boiling point, because of the pressure it's under. This super-heated water which contains a large amount of dissolved minerals, shoots out from submarine geysers called "black smokers".

Laura resonates with this energy. The heat surges through her. The minerals must be health-giving.

Around the edges of the 'black smokers', life thrives, beginning with primitive bacteria, which are the basis of the food chain. These micro-organisms generate their own food, without sunlight, from the nutrients supplied by the 'black smoker'. The species which live here aren't known to occur anywhere else in the sea.

The invertebrates that are found here include clams and mussels and giant tubeworms. The latter live on the sides of the geyser, looking like chimneys, where the water is so hot that it would kill most other creatures.

Laura was taught that the Gates to the Garden of Eden are barred by angels with flaming swords. However, she believes that this doesn't mean you can't go in. It just means that to enter, you go through the fire. Is this fire metaphorical?

The total number of different species on and around the "black smokers" is more than 300. These include small prawns, crabs and eel-like fish. These habitats are inaccessible to predators.

Some other places have underwater lakes of super-concentrated brine. These lakes have shores encrusted with thousands of mussels, ripples on the surface as well as fish swimming. They also have large beds of tubeworms. There is a whole ecosystem built on bacteria, which manage to generate food, without sunlight, from sulphides. Laura has finished rubbing her shell.

In the dark, in the Silence as well as the cold, Laura is aware of sea creatures around her. By degrees, they all take on a golden colour. At first, this is only a few spots, then patches, then full coloration. The very water, all around, becomes shimmering gold. Laura almost stops breathing. In complete stillness, Laura is overwhelmed with awe and wonder.

Emergence

Laura stands up, then walks out of the ocean. Golden water, which shimmers on her arms as well as on her body, drips from her in shining drops.

The stillness inside her seems to overflow. There is peace everywhere together with soft purity. Laura almost stops breathing. She is Silent.

How will this new state affect her relationship with Daphne? Somehow, this doesn't seem to be the question any more. Laura is whole, independent as well as self-sufficient. She stands straight. She doesn't need anyone else any more.

Giggling, dancing Nereides are singing in the distance. Daphne steps out of the water, onto the beach, a little way further up.

Laura remembers that Daphne likes her poems.

She did call me a Poet of the Sea.

With serenity, Laura turns her head, looking towards Daphne. Laura smiles.

Bibliography

Gilpin, Daniel, 2011, Ocean: Discover the Beauty of our Underwater World, Parragon, Bath U.K.

9th National Shell Show, Goodwood Community Centre, 32-34 Rosa St, Goodwood sashellclub@gmail.com

Elgar's *Sea Pictures*

Wikipedia